WEST ON THE WAGON TRAIN

THE ADVENTURES OF
YOUNG BUFFALO BILL

WEST ON THE WAGON TRAIN

BY E. CODY KIMMEL

ILLUSTRATED BY SCOTT SNOW

HARPERCOLLINS*PUBLISHERS*

Grateful acknowledgments and thanks to
Mark Bureman of the Leavenworth County
Historical Society

West on the Wagon Train
Text copyright © 2003 by E. Cody Kimmel
Illustrations copyright © 2003 by Scott Snow
address HarperCollins Children's Books, a division of HarperCollins
Publishers, 1350 Avenue of the Americas, New York, NY 10019.
www.harperchildrens.com

Library of Congress Cataloging-in-Publication Data
Kimmel, E. Cody.
  West on the wagon train / by E. Cody Kimmel ; illustrated by
Scott Snow.
    p.   cm.— (The adventures of young Buffalo Bill ; 4)
  Summary: Following the death of his father, Bill joins a wagon
train to the west, where he is befriended by the famous marksman
Wild Bill Hickok.
  ISBN 0-06-029113-3 — ISBN 0-06-029114-1 (lib. bdg.)
  1. Buffalo Bill, 1846–1917—Childhood and youth—Juvenile
fiction. [1. Buffalo Bill, 1846–1917—Childhood and youth—Fiction.
2. Hickok, Wild Bill, 1837–1876—Fiction. 3. Overland journeys to
the Pacific—Fiction.] I. Snow, Scott, ill. II. Title.
PZ7.K56475 We 2003   2002010378
[Fic]—dc21   CIP
                                                         AC

Typography by Andrea Vandergrift
1 2 3 4 5 6 7 8 9 10
❖
First Edition

★ ★ ★ ★ ★

In loving memory of James Richard Kimmel, Jr.
"Onward as thou wert wont, thou noble heart!"
—Sir James Douglas

★ ★ ★ ★ ★

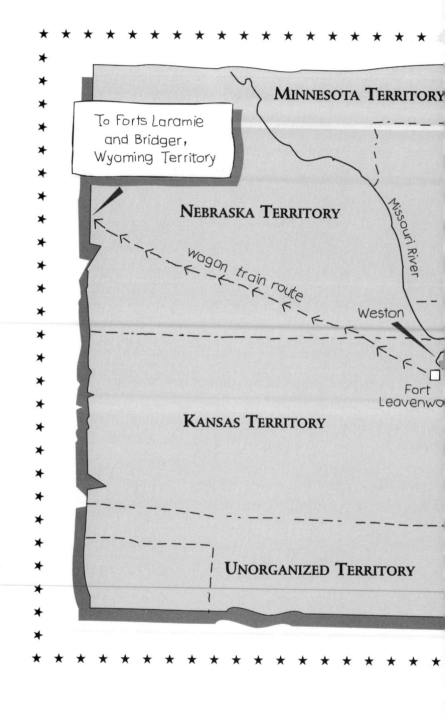

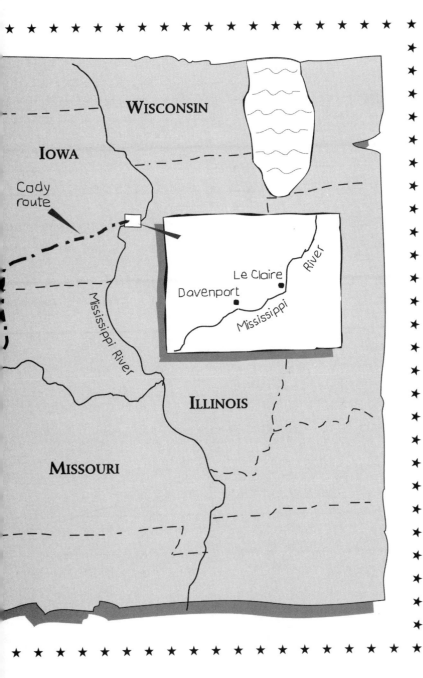

WISCONSIN

IOWA

Cody
route

Le Claire

Davenport

Mississippi River

Mississippi River

River

ILLINOIS

MISSOURI

CONTENTS

★ ★ ★ ★ ★

CHAPTER ONE

THE WAGONER'S OATH

★　　★　　★

G o ahead, son. Sign it."

Bill stared at the paper in front of him. He could not explain to Mr. Majors the sudden paralysis that had overtaken his right hand and most of his arm.

"Maybe he can't read it, Alexander," said one of the wagon masters, looking out of place in the neat office in his frayed buckskin and drooping hat.

"I'll read it to him," the wagon master continued. "All it says, son, is 'We the undersigned wagon masters,

assistants (that'd be you, Bill), teamsters, and all other employees of the firm of Majors and Russell do hereby pledge not to use profane language, not to get drunk, not to gamble, not to treat animals cruelly, and not to do anything else that is incompatible with the conduct of a gentleman.' We all signed it when we started out. Or made an X, anyhow."

Bill wanted to say loudly that he could read and he could write. He wanted Mr. Majors to know he was smart enough. But it wouldn't do to look as if he were making too much of himself. The other bull-whackers might not like that. So he said nothing, and simply leaned over the desk and carefully signed his name: William Frederick Cody.

"Well now," said Mr. Majors, glancing at the paper before folding it and putting it away. "That's done, then. Welcome to Majors and Russell, Bill. I'm sure you'll be a good worker."

"What . . ." Bill began hesitantly. Mr. Majors looked at him expectantly. "What happens now?" Bill asked. "Where do I go?"

Mr. Majors laughed. "Nowhere till morning. But you'll be with Lew Simpson. He's a good man, as I'm sure John Willis here will agree," he said, nodding toward the wagon master who'd read the wagoner's oath to Bill.

"That he is," Willis said. "You'll be hauling freight to Fort Bridger, and herding beef cattle up to Fort Kearny on the way."

"Can't imagine what this Army of Utah thinks it's gonna be fighting, with all the supplies they've ordered," Mr. Majors said. "But it sure makes for good business."

"They're expecting more trouble from the Mormons than the Indians," Mr. Willis said. Mr. Majors shrugged.

"I don't care if they're expecting trouble from the prairie dogs. The more supplies they need, the more work we have. Will you be heading home, Bill, to say good–bye to your family?"

Bill shook his head. "No sir," he added, not wanting to seem rude. He didn't explain any further. An important man like Alexander Majors didn't need to hear that Bill simply couldn't face his family again, that the last good-bye had nearly done him in, that he just needed to get on with it now and head west with a job to do.

"Suit yourself," Mr. Majors said. "You can bunk down with the other men, if you've a mind to."

"Thank you, sir," Bill said. He picked up his sack.

"I am sorry about your pa, son," Mr. Majors added. "He was a good man, as I hear tell."

Bill froze. Then he gave a stiff nod, which might have been rude but it was all he could manage. He would not think about Pa being dead. He had focused every ounce of strength he had on getting this job to make money for his family. And now he would give his entire concentration to his trip out west. He would not allow himself a minute, a second, in any day to dwell on Pa. That was not how a man acted. There could be no looking back now.

Bill reached Fort Leavenworth before sunset that evening. The wagons were being loaded from the storehouses at the fort. He already knew that most of the teamsters were camping right by the wagons outside the fort, sleeping under the open sky. Bill figured that was good enough for him. He was actually looking forward to it. The Cody cabin had seemed to grow smaller and smaller in the last months. During the two-mile walk north to Fort Leavenworth, Bill kept thinking there wasn't enough open space in Kansas left for him.

Bill had never seen so many wagons in his life as there were at Fort Leavenworth. Bill had heard Mr. Majors tell John Willis he was sending a total of forty-one wagon trains over the plains, some to stop at Fort Laramie or Fort Kearny before continuing on to supply the Army of Utah. Each train contained twenty-five wagons, and each wagon required its own ox team and its own bullwhacker, or driver. To Bill the "bull outfit," as the men called it, looked like an army all to itself—a tremendous force of man, animal, and vehicles. The area resembled a beehive, crawling with activity, men scurrying back and forth with purpose.

Bill walked toward the crowd, his few belongings slung in a sack over his shoulder. He recognized the hulking figure of Lew Simpson, the wagon master, who was supervising the loading of one of the wagons. Simpson was tall, broad, and muscled, with dark, shoulder-length hair and a thick mustache. He wore high boots with spurs, a weathered wide-brimmed hat, and rough but strong-looking trousers and shirt. Wherever he moved, men turned to acknowledge him.

Bill had never met Mr. Simpson, who would be his boss on the trip over the plains. But he had seen him in the Leavenworth office, and he'd heard plenty about the wagon master. Some said he was a rough character, and that he'd killed at least one man on every freighting trip he'd ever made. Word was that any bullwhacker, sometimes called a teamster, who got on Simpson's wrong side was in for a long and miserable haul over the plains. But a man who did his job well and without complaint could expect to be treated fairly. And on the long stretches of empty country, where hundreds of miles lay between forts or any sign of civilization, no man wanted a shrinking violet in command. Simpson could handle whatever the plains threw at him. At least, that's what Bill had overheard. He'd had to take information in little eavesdropped nuggets, as it wouldn't do to have the wagon master hear that Bill had been snooping around and asking after him.

Bill's job on the wagon train would be "extra hand." He had worked hard to get it. Ma had agreed readily enough a few months ago when Bill had asked to work as a messenger boy for Mr. Majors. He brought home ten dollars every month, money the Codys desperately needed. And most nights he slept at home, as he always had. But running messages between the Leavenworth City office and the fort was boring. Boys not much older than himself worked as assistants on the freighting missions over the plains, and the pay was twenty-five dollars a month! At first Ma refused. Bill would have to be gone for months at a time, working with men of unknown character, and exposed to all sorts of dangers. Ma would just not have it.

But Bill had developed a powerful will, and he pushed and pressed on the subject. It got so his sisters would all leave the room the instant he raised the matter. Little by little he began to wear Ma down. And when Uncle Elijah arrived for a visit, and told Ma he thought it was the right thing for Bill, she finally gave in.

At last he could do something. And not just tiresome farmwork or boring message running. This job was a frontiersman's job, an exciting and dangerous one. It was a job someone like his cousin the rough and wild horseman Horace Billings might do. Bill realized how lucky he was to get the job. Over the plains and back again, camping under the stars every night. He knew he ought to be practically jumping up and down. But it was never possible to completely put out of his mind why he needed the job in the first place—why the Codys were in trouble and needed money.

"You there!" shouted a deep, gravelly voice. Bill spun around. Mr. Simpson was looking straight at him.

"Yes sir, Mr. Simpson?" Bill said, clear enough to be heard well but not so loud as to sound sassy.

"What's your name and what are you doing here?" Mr. Simpson said.

"My name is Bill Cody, sir. Mr. Majors hired me to be your extra hand, sir."

Mr. Simpson looked Bill over carefully, narrowing his blue eyes.

"And what exactly can you do, Bill Cody?" Mr. Simpson asked.

"I'm a good rider, sir, and I can handle a team. I can herd cattle. I can handle tools, and I can shoot a gun. And if there's something I don't know how to do, I reckon I can learn quick enough."

The wagon master gave a small smile.

"You're smart enough, I can tell that. We'll just have to see about the rest. Majors is certainly hiring 'em young this summer. I guess everyone else is already out freighting. How old *are* you, son? Twelve?"

Bill nodded. It would be a lie for only eight months, after all.

Mr. Simpson studied him for another moment, then gave him a sturdy clap on the back.

"All right, then, Bill Cody. Welcome to my outfit. I'll send George when I see him. He's the assistant wagon master, and he'll see about getting you outfitted. You'll be gettin' your own blanket and mess kit, and a mule to ride. We're off tomorrow at sunrise. You know where we're headed?"

Bill knew it about as well as he knew his own name.

"Fort Kearny, sir, and then on to Fort Bridger."

Mr. Simpson nodded, but his attention was suddenly focused elsewhere.

"Jackson! Chandless! What are you doing with them crates?" he shouted in his thunderous voice.

And before Bill knew it, he was standing alone.

Chapter Two

TENDERFOOT

★   ★   ★

Bill awakened to the sudden, startling sensation of a spider running across his face. He sat bolt upright—and slammed his head against the wagon beneath which he had slept. Bill crawled out and stood up on the grass, still damp from last night's rain. Though by the rosy color of the sunlight it looked to be just after dawn, Bill could see that the camp was already alive with activity.

The solid-gray mule that the assistant wagon master

had given Bill to ride stood tethered to the wagon. Bill gave the animal a disappointed look. Prince, Bill's magnificent horse, had been left behind with his family. Mules and oxen worked the freight trains, not horses. A little pang of regret went through Bill. Nonetheless he gave the mule, who was called Mike, a couple of solid pats on the neck. It wasn't Mike's fault he was as homely as an old cowhand.

"Cody! Stop coddling that mule and start yoking this team!"

Bill jerked his hand off Mike's back as if it had caught fire. George Woods, the assistant wagon master, had come around the other side of the wagon. Bill was anxious to make a good impression on the teamsters, and he kicked himself for not being more attentive.

"Yes sir," Bill barked. A respectful response given clearly went a long way in his favor, Bill had already discovered.

Woods simply stood, staring at Bill. The assistant wagon master was tall and bony thin, with a thick shock of black hair atop a sharp-featured face. With no further instructions coming, Bill sprang into action.

The hardwood yokes were lying on the grass by the wagon, and the oxen who made up the team for this wagon were grazing lazily around them. They seemed not to know or care that their workday was about to begin.

Bill had had plenty of experience on the Cody

claim yoking ox teams by himself. Within several minutes he had the first pair done, the yoke fitting neatly over the necks, against the humps of the oxen's shoulders and the hickory bows fastened beneath their necks with a steel cotter pin. The enormous horned animals were surprisingly docile, and they responded immediately to Bill's soft words and the gentle slaps he gave on their necks to move them closer to the yoke. The animals seemed to know what was expected of them, and before long Bill had all the teams yoked.

Still Woods said nothing. So Bill led each pair one by one to the pivoted piece of wood between the front wheels of the freighter wagon. Lifting the chain on the front of the tongue, he attached it through each yoke, then stood back. The teams were now attached to the wagon. Then Bill checked the brake on the wagon, which was on. Finally he turned to look at the assistant wagon master.

Woods nodded slowly. "You'll do," he said. "Get yourself about, now, and go from wagon to wagon. The boys all know who you are, even if you don't know them. Where you see somebody needs help, or you hear an order being shouted out, you step to, understand?"

"Yes sir," Bill said. Woods looked satisfied.

"You'll do," he repeated. He gave Bill a curious look, as if he wanted to ask him something. Then he turned on his bony legs and headed up toward the quartermaster's depot.

Bill took a moment to let out a great sigh of relief. Everything had gone perfectly so far. Both the wagon master and the assistant seemed to like him. He hadn't made any mistakes or done anything embarrassing. He was going to do all right on this trip, Bill decided. He would be the best, the fastest extra hand Lew Simpson had ever had. Other than that he'd keep to himself. He didn't need or even want to make friends. Friends asked questions about your family and your past that Bill didn't want to answer. The teamsters were mostly grown men, anyway. They wouldn't bother themselves with one skinny boy.

He walked from wagon to wagon. When he saw a team that needed yoking, he yoked them. When he heard a yell for water, he ran to fetch it. If a crate was being loaded, Bill got his hands under a corner and helped. Bill saw and heard nothing but what was right in front of him. There was always something to do.

Bill had just run a bucket of water to a bullwhacker named Phelps, and was standing there waiting to reclaim his bucket as Phelps drank thirstily. Suddenly he heard shouts, and a series of sharp cracks that sounded like gunfire. He stiffened. Was the train being attacked before even getting underway?

Phelps slurped down the last of his water, belched, and grinned at Bill.

"Don't worry, tenderfoot, ain't nobody fighting us," he said. A relieved expression crossed Bill's face, and Phelps laughed.

Bill didn't like being called a tenderfoot, though as the youngest and most inexperienced hand on the train he knew that was what he was. But he wasn't going to embarrass himself further by asking what the noises were. Luckily, Phelps answered the unasked question.

"Them's the blacksnakes cracking," Phelps said. He handed Bill the bucket and picked up his own blacksnake, a long, dangerous-looking whip with a leather handle. "When you hear that sound, you know it's time to roll."

Sure enough, Bill could see that the first wagons in the train had already started to move onto the trail, their bullwhackers walking on the left side of the teams, shouting commands and cracking the whips high in the air. He grabbed his bucket and ran back to the wagon where Mike was tethered. The bullwhacker for that wagon, a man called Green, was checking the yokes on his teams. He glanced at Bill and gave him a slight nod.

Bill nodded back, fastening the girth on Mike's saddle. He'd been looking forward to this moment for so long, but now he could hardly enjoy it. The departure was too rushed, and Bill barely had time to roll his belongings inside his blanket and lash it to the back of Mike's saddle before Green's wagon, the last in the train, lurched forward. With a quick movement he was in the saddle and riding to one side of the wagon.

The train stretched out like a white snake in front of him, twenty-five wagons rolling forward, dipping and leaning over the uneven prairie. The wagons creaked and occasionally clattered, and the soft tread of the oxen's hooves on the trail was quiet and re-assuring. Every minute or so a crack split the air as a bullwhacker flicked his whip. Bill noticed the blacksnakes didn't actually touch the oxen. Instead, the whips were cracked over the animals' heads, and the sound alone was enough to cause them to pick up their pace.

Some of the teamsters began to sing.

"I'll tell you how it is when you first get on the road—
You have an awkward team and a very heavy load.
You have to whip and holler, but swear upon the sly.
You're in for it then, boys, root hog or die!"

I'm in for it now, Bill thought with satisfaction. I'm a teamster, a freighter, heading west to the forts. This is the life I've always wanted.

Bill found himself imagining how he would describe the scene to his sister Julia. He pictured all his sisters gathered around him, Julia looking admiring and envious, and Nellie squealing with delight when he described the crack of the blacksnakes. Martha might shake her head in disapproval of this rough men's work. Eliza Alice wouldn't stop her mending for a moment, except maybe to shudder at the thought of spending a whole summer out of doors. Mary Hannah would want to know who the bad guys were, and whether there were any Indians. Little Charlie would play his two-year-old version of cowboys 'n' injuns.

And Ma. What would Ma say? She would worry, first of all. All those oxen that might stampede for any reason. The high probability that bathing and toothbrushing were not taking place with any frequency. The coarseness of the language (in spite of the fact that they all had to promise Mr. Majors they would not swear).

But she would be proud, too. She might not say so. But Bill knew he would see pride in his mother's eyes, and admiration of the boy who had been working like a man since he was eight years old. A boy who had always faced his responsibilities, now more than ever since Pa had . . .

Bill abruptly shook himself out of the daydream. These were things he had promised not to think about. Were all these bullwhackers dreaming of their families as they walked alongside their teams, cracking their blacksnakes? Were they feeling sad and sorry for themselves over people they'd lost? Bill would bet a week's pay they weren't. And if he was one of them now, he couldn't dwell on such things either.

Though most of Bill's duties as extra hand would take place when the train was stopped, or camped out for the night, Bill had also been told to make himself available as they were rolling. So he urged Mike forward, trotting past Green and his wagon and slowly making his way forward toward the head of the train, almost a quarter mile in the distance. As he passed the wagons, most of the bullwhackers acknowledged him with a nod or a word.

Then he rode past a stocky, sour-faced bullwhacker in old, dirty clothes. The brim of his hat was fastened back with a wooden pin. Bill nodded at the man, but when the bullwhacker caught sight of him, his already surly face took on a glower, and he spat on the ground right where Bill was riding.

Shocked, Bill gave Mike a nudge to speed him up. The next bullwhacker he passed gave a friendly wave. Bill waved back, but he was still shaken. Why had that bullwhacker spat at him? What had he done wrong? He continued making his way up the line, greeting each teamster in turn, but he had a sense of worry that he had not had before.

Eventually Bill reached the front of the line, and he could see Mr. Simpson riding out front, the only man in the outfit with a horse. A wagon master needed to move ahead of the mules, to scout for a suitable place to break, but to be on the lookout for danger as well. Bill hadn't heard any stories of Indian problems this summer, but there were plenty of other things that might harm a wagon train. Mud holes, snake dens, an approaching herd of buffalo. Bad weather. It all had to be anticipated and, if possible, avoided. Bill watched Simpson, sitting ramrod straight on his horse and scanning the landscape for something or other. Bill knew that every bullwhacker aspired to be a wagon master like Mr. Simpson. Masters were respected, feared, and handsomely paid. A wagon master had to know everything, from doctoring sick men and animals to sweet-talking Indians. Bill thought he might make a decent wagon master himself, some day, if only he could get a little bigger and stronger.

Now Mr. Simpson had stopped. He turned back and looked right at Bill, as if he knew the boy had been following him. Bill gave Mike a quick kick and rode toward Mr. Simpson as fast as he could without looking eager. As soon as he was within hearing distance, the wagon master said, "We'll break here. Yonder is enough good grazing for the oxen, and over by that copse of trees is a decent stream. Pass the word."

"Yes sir," Bill called, happy to have such important and welcome news to tell.

★ 17 ★

He rode back the way he'd come, down the line of wagons.

"Noon halt," he called. "Stopping ahead. Noon halt—stopping ahead."

Bill's stomach tightened as he approached the surly bullwhacker's wagon. To his relief he saw George Woods already there.

"Mr. Simpson says noon halt ahead," Bill said to Mr. Woods. He knew the bullwhacker could hear him, and this way he didn't have to address him directly. Mr. Woods nodded.

"You'll need to help get the teams unhitched, Bill, and drive them to the water before they graze. Then get over to your mess wagon and help out with the grub."

"Yes sir," Bill said. He headed toward the next wagon, but not before hearing the sullen bullwhacker imitating his "yes sir" in a high, girlish voice, and the sounds of both men laughing.

By the time the oxen had drunk their fill and had been led to the grazing area, Bill was almost weak with hunger. The train was divided into three messes of around ten men each, and Bill made his way between the three groups, delivering water and wood he'd collected for the fire. Each mess elected its own cook and was responsible for preparing its own food. Soon the smell of frying bacon and brewing coffee filled the air, and the sight of Green stirring beans in the skillet made Bill's eyes almost pop out of his head. Green saw Bill's face and tossed him an apple, which Bill devoured gratefully as he hauled the water keg back to the stream.

It seemed as if hours passed before he finally had a tin plate of bacon and beans in front of him. Trying not to look as famished as he felt, he carried his plate to a quiet place near one of the wagons. He sat down and put a whole piece of bacon in his mouth. Just as the delicious, fatty taste spread across his tongue, he felt a tremendous and painful blow on his back. The bacon in his mouth flew out, and the contents of his plate dumped onto the grass. As Bill tried to catch his breath and find out what had attacked him, he heard the sound of a gravelly, sullen laugh. The now-familiar broad back of the ill-tempered bullwhacker passed him by.

When he recovered his breath, he began to collect his bacon and beans, picking the bits of grass off as best he could. A cheerful-looking blond man who was walking by paused to take note of Bill's scattered food.

"Looks like Clayton Ewell got the best of you, son," the man said, not without sympathy. Bill nodded.

"Try not to pay him any mind. That man don't have one funny bone in his whole body. I snuck a toad into his coffee once, and he near took my head off. I do despise a man who can't tolerate a good joke. Hank Bassett's the name," he added.

"Bill Cody," Bill replied, and Hank nodded.

"Yup. Well, good hunting," Hank said, and walked off.

Bill felt thoroughly miserable that on his very first dinner break of his very first day out on the plains, he was reduced to picking boiled beans out of the grass.

He hoped no one else saw.

CHAPTER THREE
WILD BILL

★   ★   ★

Within three days the routine was already familiar. The entire outfit rose at dawn, and Bill's first job was to help herd the oxen that had been grazing overnight. Once the oxen were delivered to the correct wagons, they had to be yoked and hitched. Blankets and mess items had to be stowed away, camp fires kicked out, and the wagons checked to make sure each crate was still safely lashed down.

They had no real breakfast, which Bill was still trying to get used to. Sometimes Green had a little cold coffee or a bit of biscuit to pass out, but Bill's stomach was usually growling by the time the train got rolling. They would travel until almost noon, when Mr. Simpson would find them a break spot. There the oxen would be let loose to graze while the men ate their main meal of the day. Green explained to Bill that the more grass the oxen ate during this dinner hour, the less hungry they'd be during the night. They'd sleep instead of spending the night grazing. That made for a refreshed and even-tempered animal come daylight.

Since leaving Fort Leavenworth they had been heading roughly northwest over the prairie, making about fifteen miles a day. When they eventually reached the Platte River in Nebraska Territory, probably in two and a half weeks, they would follow it west to Fort Kearny. They would continue following the North Platte River some three hundred miles to Fort Laramie, and finally leave the river and head southwest for their final destination of Fort Bridger, some hundred miles from Salt Lake City.

In addition to the twenty-five wagons of supplies for the Army of Utah, the train was also driving a thousand head of beef cattle, which would be delivered to Fort Kearny to feed the troops stationed there.

They made camp the third evening on a high swell

of prairie just a quarter mile from a tree-lined stream. Here they could provide themselves with fresh water and firewood, and weather permitting, they could lay their blankets right on the grass, under the open wide sky.

Bill immediately started hauling firewood. The wood had to be fetched first, before the water, so that each mess could get a good fire burning. He had hauled several loads of kindling and two kegs of water back to his cookfire when Green said, "Bill, I'll need you to make the bread. I got my hands full."

"Yes sir," Bill said quickly, deciding immediately that it would be a mistake to tell Green he didn't know how to make bread. Green handed Bill a dishpan already filled with flour.

"The Dooleys is yonder," Green said, making a gesture with his head, and then he walked away. Bill swallowed nervously. The meals of ten men, and Bill's entire reputation, hung in the balance. Bill desperately called an image of Julia to his mind, and cursed all the days he had stood by while she baked and not paid a whit of attention to what she was doing.

Dooleys. Bill could remember Julia talking about Dooleys. It was some kind of powder you put in bread and cakes to make them rise. Too little and it didn't work. Too much, as Bill remembered from one of Nellie's "baking" experiments, made the bread bitter. Think, Bill said to himself. He could see Julia clearly, chattering and standing by the table mixing flour and water together in a bowl. He remembered a particular argument they had once had during baking, when Julia said that if Prince were let loose to run wild with the Indian ponies, he would forget Bill within the month and spend out his days happy and free on the plains.

Bill had rolled his eyes and told Julia that was a load of claptrap, and that he hoped she knew more about baking than horses. He informed her that the bond he and Prince had was as powerful as that between Ma and Baby Charlie. He haughtily reminded her how Prince, after being stolen, had broken free from his captors and never stopped running till he got back to the Codys' stables. Julia had harrumphed at that, suggested Prince just knew where to find a good meal, and emphasized her statement by dumping a handful of Dooleys into the baking bowl.

A handful of Dooleys. He picked up the little burlap sack Green had shown him and reached inside it. He put a handful of the powder in the bowl. He carried it to the creek and mixed in water until it looked about the way Julia's dough had. He carried the dough back to the cookfire, where Green had left a little dutch oven, in the bottom of which sat a piece of bacon fat. Well, at least Bill knew what to do with *that*. He rubbed it all along the sides until they were good and greased. Then he plopped the dough in, covered the pot, and set it on top of the fire to cook, placing some coals over the lid so the bread would bake evenly.

It was not the finest bread Bill had ever eaten. It was singed on the outside and doughy in the middle. Still, it was definitely bread, and the men ate it without comment. What would Ma say? With all her worrying about the bad influences Bill might encounter on the bull train, here he was doing women's work!

The temperature had cooled, and it felt wonderfully clear. It was nice to take deep breaths without gulping down the dust that the rolling wagons and oxen constantly churned into the air. Overhead, the moon had risen and became brighter as the last of the sunlight faded. For a time things seemed peaceful as the men ate in quiet. Then a harsh voice broke the silence.

"Tenderfoot! Fetch me another coffee—this here tastes like coffin varnish."

It was the bullwhacker who had spat at him and hit him, the man Hank Bassett had called Clayton Ewell. Bill was already on his feet, though he did not fully understand what Ewell wanted. The coffee had all come from the same pot, which still contained some bubbling muddy-looking liquid. Did Ewell want more of the same, or was he expecting Bill to make a new pot?

"Dammit, are you deaf? Fetch the coffee, you oaf!"

Bill glanced over at Green, but the bullwhacker merely shrugged and continued eating. He was obviously used to this, and saw no reason to interrupt his meal to get involved. Suddenly, Ewell was on his feet and charging toward Bill. He delivered Bill such a powerful slap across the head that the boy went sprawling, prone, on the ground.

His ears ringing, Bill jumped back up immediately, dodging the savage kick Ewell had aimed at him. Bill noticed that, like Green, the other men were hardly paying any attention at all. Fights were commonplace, and if one of the participants was only twelve (almost), well, that was life on the bull train. Bill knew that he was on his own, though he was completely outweighed, outmuscled, and outpowered by the angry bullwhacker.

Ewell had one arm raised, his hand curled tightly into a fist. If he delivered this blow, Bill knew he might not be able to get up a second time. He looked around for a weapon and found nothing. Ewell advanced, and in a split second Bill reached toward the fire, grabbed the pot of coffee, and hurled the remainder of the hot liquid across Ewell's neck and chest. Ewell howled like an animal, took a moment to rip his shirt away from his skin, then launched himself at Bill with the ferocity of a wounded grizzly bear.

I'm dead, was all Bill had time to think as he braced himself. He heard a thud, and the sound of an *oof* of air coming out of someone's lungs, followed by the thump of someone's body hitting the ground.

Bill looked down at himself. He was standing, whole and unhurt. Clayton Ewell lay sprawled on his back, rubbing a cut on his head that had begun to bleed heavily.

"What in hell did you do that for?" Ewell demanded. "You got no business puttin' your oar in here!"

For a second Bill thought Ewell was talking to him, though he knew he had not laid a hand on the man.

"It's my business to protect that boy, or anybody else, from being unmercifully abused, kicked, and cuffed, and I'll whip you or any man who tries it," came a cool voice.

Bill looked around, trying to locate his savior. There he was, leaning against a wagon wheel. Bill had noticed this man before. He had a face that was hard to take your eyes from. He was long and lean, with wavy dark hair tucked behind his ears and falling to his shoulders. His face was all lines and angles, his nose long and straight, and his brown eyes sloped slightly downward toward his cheekbones, giving him somewhat of a sad expression. He was what his sister Martha undoubtedly would have called, with a slight intake of breath, "a fine-looking man." The man noticed Bill staring at him and gave the boy a little wink.

Bill gave a little nod in return, torn between his embarrassment at having to be rescued from a fight and gratitude that someone had stepped in to save his hide.

"You remember what I said, now, Ewell," the man said as he turned to walk away. "Or I'll give you a pounding you won't get over for a month of Sundays."

Ewell was still sitting on the ground, and he remained there as the man who'd beaten him strode off into the darkness. Then he turned to Bill and gave him such a look of hatred that Bill's insides went cold.

"Now Clayton," said Green, who had never stopped eating this whole time. "Heed what the man said, and let's have no more of it."

Ewell said nothing—simply spat on the ground, and walked away. A few of the men chuckled.

"You made yourself one powerful friend today," said one of the bullwhackers, a man named Ferd. "I don't think Clayton Ewell will dare bother you after tonight. Or anyone else, once word gets out."

"I don't know," Bill said. "I ain't got a clue what I've done to make him hate me so."

"You're a tenderfoot, and a Yankee too if my hearing ain't failing me," said Ferd. "Clayton can't even look at a tenderfoot without whacking him upside the head, and he comes from a long line of Yankee haters. You *are* a Yankee, ain't you, boy?"

"My family came from Iowa before we settled in Kansas Territory," Bill said.

Ferd nodded. "Well, there you have it. But don't fret over it, young Bill. Even Clayton Ewell ain't stupid enough to make trouble for you *now*."

"Why?" Bill asked, sitting back down on the ground and retrieving his supper.

Ferd laughed, and a few other men joined in.

"Why, son, don't you know who that fella was? The one who decked Clayton? Don't you recognize him?"

Mystified, Bill shook his head, and now all the men roared with laughter.

"That was Wild Bill Hickok, pup! And there ain't no man in this outfit or any other that's gonna cross him and hope to stay alive."

Wild Bill Hickok. Although Bill had never heard the name before, the sound of it sent a little thrill through his body.

"They say," said Ferd, leaning toward Bill and lowering his voice, "that Wild Bill Hickok is the deadest pistol shot alive. They say no man what crossed him ever lived to tell the tale. They say"—here Ferd dropped his voice to a whisper—"they say he'd shoot his own grandma if she looked at him wrong."

"I knew a gunfighter once, years back," said a wiry bullwhacker named Hiram. "In Missouri. Dead Eye Jim, they called him. You wouldn't know it to look at him—he was a scrawny little fella, seemed like he might up and blow away if the wind picked up. But he didn't take no lip from no one. To start out he was just a gambler. Didn't look for no trouble unless it came looking for him. But then one day he turned outlaw. Don't no one know why. Some say he got spurned by a girl. Some say he was only waiting for his ma to pass on. But whatever the reason, he got himself a gang together and started robbing banks. Dead Eye Jim didn't mean to get caught, ever, so he shot every man in every posse that ever tried to bring him in. Until one day . . ." Hiram paused and took a long drink of water.

"Until one day what?" Bill blurted out. He immediately regretted speaking up. Had he broken some kind of rule? But Hiram only nodded, as if he had been waiting for encouragement before finishing.

"Until one day, during a getaway, Dead Eye Jim and his boys got themselves backed into a blind canyon. Every direction but one was rock, straight up, and the sheriff what was chasing them blocking the way out with his posse. Dead Eye's boys gave themselves up straightaway, and rode out with their hands over their heads, 'bout as brave as a gang of milkmaids. But Dead Eye wouldn't go. Fired every shot in his six-shooter before they got him. Guess he figured he was done for anyway, and he'd rather die like a gunfighter than swing at the end of a rope like any old horsethief."

"Reckon old Dead Eye should have stuck to card playing," said Ferd.

"Well that may be," said Hiram, "that may be. But if he had, I don't reckon we'd be sittin' around the fire tellin' his story, would we? Nobody wants to hear about Dead Eye Jim, the peaceable gambler."

Just one month ago Bill had been eating Ma's stew and Julia's bread, doing farm chores, and running messages. And now he was on the plains under the open sky, eating stew by a campfire and listening to stories about gunfighters. He could hardly believe it was all real. And even better, Wild Bill Hickok, deadest pistol shot alive, had stood up for Bill in a fight. The thrill of it was still fresh, but after what he'd just heard about Dead Eye Jim, Bill wondered if Wild Bill was . . . safe.

"Now you spooked the boy, Hiram," said Ferd, sounding pleased about it. "Don't you worry about Wild Bill, son. He's no outlaw."

"At least not so far," added Hiram ominously.

CHAPTER FOUR

STORM TIMES

★ ★ ★

The storm came fierce and swift, sweeping across the plains and pummeling the outfit with all of nature's majestic indifference to man and beast. Not an hour earlier Bill had been hot beyond limit, his throat burning from the dusty air and his skin cured like a buffalo hide beneath the relentless July sun. Bill hated the days when he was told to ride at the rear of the train, where the

swirling dirt kicked up by two hundred oxen and twenty-five wagons collected around him, seeping into his ears, his nose, through his clothes. His view was a wall of brown with an occasional glimpse of Green's wagon in front of him. Just as he thought he couldn't stand it another moment, he became aware of a darkening overhead, and of a black shadow advancing toward them, swallowing landscape as it came.

They had come over two hundred miles in two weeks, and Bill had thought by now they had encountered every extreme of weather the plains had to offer, from crackling displays of lightning to hot dust storms. But those had been nothing but games, Bill realized, compared to what was headed toward them now.

If orders were being shouted, Bill could not hear them over the wind. The first fat raindrops splattered down, and within minutes the dust began to settle. Now Bill could see the wagons pulling into a circle, and the beef cattle being herded into their center. Bill dismounted, unsaddled Mike, and tethered him to Green's wagon, tossing the saddle beneath it. Green

had already unhitched his team, so Bill ran on, pulling his hat over his face to shield it from the black sheets of rain and trying to make out the figures of Mr. Simpson or George Woods to see if there was anything he should be doing. The sky was now completely black overhead, ripped through constantly by lightning. The thunder made a constant, growing roar like the sound of stampeding animals.

Something sharp hit Bill on the back of the hand, landing a stinging blow. He made the mistake of turning his face up to the sky to see where the missile had come from. Another struck him low on the forehead, drawing blood before bouncing to the ground. Hail, was all Bill had time to think, before the assault began in earnest. White frozen balls rained down all around him, exploding like gunshot as they hit the ground. They hit him everywhere—his back, his shoulders, the backs of his legs. They gathered in the brim of his hat. The ones that struck his bare skin cut little welts into him.

Bill ducked his head down. He realized there was nothing he could do to help but take shelter, and now he was worried about leaving Mike untended. Bill struggled back in the direction he guessed he'd left Green's wagon. Either his guess was better than he'd thought or he was due for a spell of blind luck. Whatever the reason, Green's wagon was the first Bill reached. Mike was standing with his hindquarters to the wind and his head down. Bill got his blanket out of the wagon and threw it over the animal's back. He knew there wasn't anything else he could do for the mule.

Bill crawled underneath the wagon. Though the wagon gave little relief from the wind, Bill found that if he pressed himself right up against the wheel, almost none of the hailstones could reach him. Pulling his hat as far down around his ears as he could get it, Bill hunched over and steeled himself against the storm.

The wind continued to blow harder. One minute it sounded like a steam whistle, the next like a chorus of wailing girls. The sound chilled Bill's bones. He shivered, wrapping his arms around himself and pulling his knees up to his chin. It was then that he noticed he was not alone beneath the wagon. A figure was crouched by the back wheel, a dark shadow that coughed occasionally. Bill doubted any man had a voice loud enough to be heard over the wind. He certainly did not. And this was no time for talk, anyway. So he simply took note of the other person's presence and felt comforted by the company.

The wagon wheel shifted against Bill's back. The canvas on the wagon was acting as a sail, and the wind caused it to strain and shudder. The brakes were on, and each wagon was chained to the next, but if the wind chose to move the wagon, nothing would stop it. Then, as if it had read Bill's thoughts, the wind suddenly gusted, and the wagon shuddered as the wheel lifted several inches off the ground.

It's going to tip, Bill thought. And it'll pull Mike right over with it. The wheel came down with a thud, then lifted again as another gust hit the canvas. This time it went a good ten inches into the air. Bill reached up and wrapped his arms around one of the supports, then snaked his legs up as well, so he was clinging to the beam like a baby to its mama. He knew he didn't weigh much, but maybe it was just enough to make the difference in preventing the wagon from tipping over. Bill hung on for all he was worth, as the wagon tipped and landed, tipped and landed, never getting much more than a foot off the ground. At some point Bill became aware that the other person had joined him in holding the wagon down. Bill thought he could hear the sound of chuckling. Or maybe it was just another trick of the wind.

Then the wind fell away abruptly, and the wagon settled firmly into the mud. Gingerly Bill let himself down and stretched his aching limbs. The man who'd held the wagon next to him was gone. The hailstones had stopped falling, and it was just raining now, the drops making a hissing sound as they landed. The last thing Bill remembered thinking was that it sounded like a giant pan of frying bacon. He comforted himself with the thought of a prairie-sized fry pan cooking up a slice of pig as big as a stagecoach. Then, against all reasonable possibilities, Bill fell asleep.

Looking across the plains, it was as if the storm had never happened. The sky was a brilliant blue, and the summer sun burned hotly onto the rippling prairie. But one glance at the wagon train gave plenty of evidence of the storm that had passed. The canvas on many of the wagons was ripped and shredded. Several wagons had been blown over, breaking their chains and spilling their crated contents onto the ground. Men fanned out on foot, hunting down the cattle that had run off during the storm. There was much to be done before the outfit would be fit to travel again. Bill didn't bother looking for Mr. Simpson for instructions. He simply threw himself into the closest task at hand, which was collecting and repacking the supplies that had scattered out of an overturned wagon.

Several of the spilled crates had broken open. Bill worked to refill one that had been loaded with bags of nails and shot. He worked quickly on his hands and knees, going through the grass carefully to collect scattered pieces. He separated shot from nails, filled and tied each bag, and piled the sacks back into their crates. Then he left them. Bill knew that no crate was ever closed and loaded onto a wagon without being inspected and approved by the wagon master, who was responsible for every item being shipped.

Bill went from job to job, losing all track of time until he heard a familiar and welcome song:

"Bacon in the pan,
Coffee in the pot,
Come up and get it—
Get it while it's hot."

No one had to hear that song twice. All around Bill, men stopped what they were doing and headed for their mess groups.

Though he'd been eating bacon and beans almost every night since leaving Fort Leavenworth, Bill attacked his food with delight. They all ate sitting in a circle around the fire, exchanging stories of who saw what during the storm, showing each other cuts and bruises and swapping tales that grew taller with every telling. Bill noticed that Clayton Ewell did not add any stories. He seemed to join in a conversation only when there was something ugly to be said.

"Young Bill," said Hank Bassett when there was a lull in the conversation. "Wild Bill Hickok says that when your wagon began to blow over, you grabbed hold and rode it like it was a crazy old mustang!"

"I guess that's right," Bill replied as the older men laughed. So it was Wild Bill under the wagon with me! was what he thought. His next thought was less pleasant. Had Wild Bill been making fun of him? Well, so what if he had? Bill thought. He had to show he could take being teased as well as the next fellow.

"Well, I don't reckon you weigh much more than a couple a prairie chickens," Hank pressed, still grinning.

Ferd interrupted. "Now be fair, Hank. The boy weighs at least four prairie chickens."

Hank laughed. "But what good are even four prairie chickens in a storm like that?"

"Well, my wagon didn't tip over, and I hear tell the one you was under did. So *you* tell me what good four prairie chickens are," Bill replied.

A shout of laughter followed his remark, and Hank laughed hardest of all, slapping his knee.

Bill felt a warmth, one that came not from the fire but from inside him. These were good men working the hardest and best job on the plains. Even though he was only a tenderfoot, and even though some of them never bothered to say a word to him, right now he felt he belonged with them. Maybe some of them, like Green and George, would always be distant and see him as only an errand boy. But the friendliness of other men like Wild Bill and Hank made Bill feel he could now hold his own in the bull outfit.

"Hey, Bill," said Hiram. "What was so all-fired important about that wagon, anyway?"

"It wasn't the wagon I was worried about," said Bill. "It was Mike."

"Mike the carpenter?" asked Hiram, confused.

"No, Mike the mule," Bill said. Hiram snorted.

"You can always trust a man who puts his animals first," came Wild Bill's voice. Bill never seemed to see him until he was about two feet away.

"Grub?" Green asked Wild Bill. Nobody ever called him Wild Bill to his face, because everybody had already heard that the last time a fellow did that, he got a whiskey glass shot clean out of his hand.

"No, thanks, had some already," Wild Bill said. He sat down next to Bill, whose ears had gone red on hearing the word *man* used to describe him. Bill spooned some beans into his mouth. Should he say hello? Or simply nod? Maybe he shouldn't speak at all. Just because Wild Bill Hickok had sat down next to him didn't mean he had an invitation to speak. It wouldn't do to look as if he were getting too big for his britches.

"Evening, Bill Cody," said Wild Bill. Bill swallowed his mouthful all at once, almost choking.

"Evening, Mr. Hickok," he replied. Wild Bill gave him a sad smile. Was he wrong to have called him Mr. Hickok? Surely he shouldn't have called him Bill! Was everyone looking at him?

But the conversation had gone right on and didn't seem to be focused in any way on how Bill had or had not addressed Wild Bill Hickok in the proper fashion.

Who was ever going to believe that a dead pistol shot named Wild Bill Hickok was working as a bull-whacker, that he'd sat down right next to Bill and said "evening" as pleasant as you please? Wild Bill was a popular topic of conversation in the outfit, and Bill had managed to learn a lot about him just by listening. He now knew that Wild Bill could shoot an apple off a tree through its stem, and then shoot clean through the center of the same apple before it hit the ground. Someone even said that one shot from his pistol could drive a cork into a bottle without breaking the glass. And Bill's favorite story was that a crazy man had once thrown a rock at the head of one of Wild Bill's friends. In the blink of an eye, Wild Bill had drawn his gun and shot that rock out of the air before it ever reached its mark.

The men were laughing at something, and Wild Bill gave a small chuckle as he leaned back comfortably against an ox yoke. Bill slid a glance at Wild Bill's hips, where his pistols were strapped, butts facing forward. No one else in the outfit carried a pistol on him, except for the wagon master. Bill wondered if Mr. Simpson had made a special exception for Wild Bill, or if the subject had never been brought up at all.

"And there'll be mail going out of Fort Kearny," Ferd was saying. "Ought to be there in a week. So we best all get to writing to our wives or sweethearts."

"Or our folks," said Hank, nodding toward Bill.

"That's right, Bill, you better start keeping an account of all your heroics now. I reckon your pa will be well-nigh pleased when he hears how you're doing, won't he?"

Bill froze where he was sitting.

"Don't tell me you're going to be one of them humble ones," Ferd continued. "'Cause if you is, I reckon I'll just have to write to your pa myself and set him straight."

"Shut pan, Ferd, and keep to your own," said Wild Bill suddenly.

"He's Isaac Cody's boy, remember?" Hank said, and Ferd slapped his hand to his forehead.

"I 'pologize, Bill. It's a damn shame what happened to your pa, and my tongue goes faster'n my memory sometimes."

Bill mumbled something, as several other men offered sympathetic remarks.

Though he tried not to show it, Bill was startled. They knew about Pa. Apparently, they all knew, every one of them. Bill had been so determined to keep his business to himself. He had sworn that he would never mention Pa to anyone, nor would he allow himself to think about him. He was here to do a man's job, and what could be less manly than getting red-eyed over something that was never going to change? And yet now he realized that his family situation was all over the outfit. Even Wild Bill Hickok had enough time between shooting apples out of the air to find out what had happened to Isaac Cody.

Maybe this was why some of them had been so nice to Bill. They were just feeling sorry for the half-orphaned boy who had to go to work to support his family. What an oaf, what a foolish tenderfoot he'd been, imagining how the teamsters would come to see him as one of their own through his hard work and even temper. No, it was pity that made them kind!

Bill didn't want to draw any attention to himself, but he had to get away. Standing up in what he hoped was a casual way, he collected a pan full of dishes and hauled them down to the stream to start washing up.

He might be the smallest toad in the puddle, but Bill was not going to let himself cry. Whenever he found himself starting to feel sad or think about Pa, Bill would force himself to think about something that made him mad instead. Now he thought about the border ruffians who'd stolen Prince from him. He pictured each one of their faces, and how their voices had sounded as they led Prince from the stable and took him away as their prize. He remembered the rage that had swept over him as he watched, unable to stop the theft. He heard the border ruffians' triumphant laughter, mingled with the sound of moving horses, as they disappeared into the night with Prince. Then Bill let himself remember how, later, Prince had broken free and returned home. Bill smiled a little. His old trick had worked—he no longer felt like crying, and the memory of Pa had been pushed away.

Bill felt he was being watched. He turned slowly, and there was Wild Bill, holding some more plates in his hands. He sat down and began to wash up. Bill sat down next to him and did the same. They worked in silence for a while.

"I came to Kansas Territory two years ago to stake a claim, after my pa died, though I wasn't yet of age," Wild Bill said. He'd finished the plates he was washing and didn't reach for any more.

"Twice my cabins were burned to the ground by pro-slavers. Finally I got so riled, I up and joined Jim Lane's army so's I could do something about it. I was born a dead shot, and I reckon it's about the only talent God gave me. I aimed to use it against gangs like the ones who tried to drive me off my claim. But they just kept coming. I expect they'll always keep coming, and I don't know what's gonna stop 'em, 'cept for a war."

It was quite something, Bill thought, what he had in common with Wild Bill. Both had come west to settle in Kansas. Both had lost their fathers. Both had been persecuted by the border ruffians. And both had joined the bull train. If Bill could share that many experiences with Wild Bill Hickok, maybe he wasn't as much of an outsider as he thought.

"So I joined up with Majors and Russell. Left my claim behind. We all lost something, left something behind," Wild Bill said, as if reading Bill's mind. "It's why we're here. And it's why we're us. My pa was a preaching man, and he used to say the measure of a man was in what he'd lost. Some might look around our outfit and see an immigrant from Sweden, or a carpenter with a quick temper, or a bullwhacker who used to ride with the ruffians himself. But they all got their stories. Maybe one of 'em lost a family to cholera, or their pa took off without a word, or they started out with nothing and had to fight for everything they ever got.

"Don't get me wrong—I'm not heaping pity on anybody," Wild Bill said, giving Bill a sidelong glance. "But when you hear a fella's story, and you understand something about what he's lost, then you can really see him. You can see he's not so different from you."

Wild Bill fell silent, and he looked as if he'd said all he was going to say on the subject.

Bill knew he wasn't talking about any one man; he was talking about all of them. Though Bill did wonder what Clayton Ewell's story might be.

They sat together in silence for a long time. Bill had finished the rest of the plates. There was a sliver of moon visible over the copse of trees, and the stars peeked out one at a time until the sky was strewn with them.

After a long time Bill said, "I don't want to sound a fool, but . . . what should I call you? Because I know I ain't supposed to call you Wild Bill—" Bill clapped his hand over his mouth. Was he even supposed to *say* Wild Bill in front of the man? Had his big mouth just ruined everything?

Wild Bill chuckled, rubbing his black mustache between two fingers.

"Best just call me James."

"James?" Bill asked, thoroughly confused. "Why do you want me to call you James?"

"Because," Wild Bill said, his eyes bright and merry in the starlight, "because that's my name."

"But then why do folks call you Wild Bill? Why don't they call you Wild James?"

"Oh, that's a story for another time," said Wild Bill.

Let this be a lesson, Bill thought to himself, that nothing is ever what it seems to be, and the best thing to do is just ask.

CHAPTER FIVE

FORT KEARNY

A t first glance Fort Kearny was not much of a fort. It was set on a heavily traveled trail following the Platte River, in Nebraska Territory. There was no wall around it to act as fortification. Five wooden buildings set in a square facing each other formed a central parade. Long rectangular houses made of sod flanked the wooden buildings. On first look it might have been a farm, or a cluster of schoolhouses. Only the sixteen blockhouse guns and the mountain howitzers set to the side of the parade indicated that the fort was equipped for defense. In April and May, when most overland expeditions were setting out, thousands upon thousands of covered wagons passed by the fort, relying on its storeroom, hospital, and mail delivery services. But there were many fewer trains coming through this late in the season, and Bill found himself the subject of many curious glances from the soldiers, though they looked pleased at the delivery of beef cattle.

"Already had one Majors and Russell train through this season," a young, unshaven private was saying as he scratched through his tangled hair with two fingers.

"Government is sending a second train to supply the Army of Utah," Bill said.

"This late in the season?" the soldier asked. "Snows come as early as September near Salt Lake. Y'all may not make it."

"I reckon Mr. Majors knows what he's doing," Bill said, a little stiffly.

"Not saying no to more money is what he's doing," said Ferd and Hank, who'd walked over to join them. They were standing on the grass by a thin copse of cottonwood trees off to one side of the main parade. Ferd took a sip from a flask and passed it around Bill to Hank. Bill could not help feeling indignant at being passed over, though he'd never tasted whiskey in his life and wasn't sure he cared to.

"Can't hardly blame Majors," Hank was saying in his cheerful way. "Got the only government contract to haul supplies, no competition from any other outfit.

When they come and ask if he can send another train out, what's he supposed to say?"

"Reckon we'll get there soon enough, anyway," said Ferd.

"You'd get there faster if you used mules," said another soldier who had joined them, as unshaven and unkempt as the private.

His comment provoked an immediate eruption of outraged noises. Hank and Ferd were the loudest.

"Balderdash!" said Hank. "Why, any teamster worth his salt knows an ox can outpull a mule any day."

"I hear mules is faster," said the private, still itching at his head.

"Faster!" shouted Ferd. "What good is faster when you're stuck in a mud hole or your wheel gets jammed halfway across the Platte? Get nowhere faster, that's what.

"Bulls is reliable, bulls is cheap, bulls is loyal," Ferd added. "They do a good day's work and gather their own food out of the prairie grass."

"I hear a mule can do as much work as an ox on a third less food, and that they almost never take sick," said a stout, red-faced soldier who was passing by and overheard the debate.

"Mule skinners say they're the only way to freight," said Itchy Head.

"Mules are like nervous old ladies, and they'll

stampede for any reason," Bill said indignantly. "I heard once of a whole team that started stampeding just because the driver's hat blew off and landed on one of their hooves. Before you knew it, the whole entire train was stampeding, bags and people falling out of the wagons all over the place."

"There you have it," said Ferd with satisfaction. But the private was unconvinced.

"Ain't what I heard . . ." Itchy Head began.

"You heard claptrap!" Hank shouted. "Don't you know that the mule is the *only* animal Noah didn't take into the ark?"

That managed to silence the lot of them. When the soldiers weren't looking, Hank winked at Bill. Bill grinned. Nothing ever seemed to affect Hank's good-natured mood. Even when he argued he stayed cheerful.

Hiram Cummings walked by holding a small sack in his hand.

"Been to see the postmaster, fellas?" Hiram asked, without slowing down.

"Well, no, we been defending ourselves," said Hank.

"Oughtta go," Hiram called over his shoulder. "Green had a whole stack of letters from his family, and a package too."

"There's time enough, I reckon," Bill said, but Hank shook his head.

"Not if you aim to write back, there ain't. Won't be another chance to mail a letter till we get to Fort Laramie. We're only here for the night, and we got the supply lists to go over with the Kearny agent. You'd best shake a leg."

Bill nodded, but he didn't get up. Part of him ached to run to the postmaster in hope of mail. He was anxious for news of his family, and to know that they were all healthy and well.

But he was afraid, too. Reading news of his family would bring them back into his circle of worry. On the bulltrain his days were consumed by concern for the beef cattle, the crust of the baking bread, the height of the cookfire, and the strength of the coffee he brewed. He worried about the weather, the oxen's hooves, and the spot on Mike's back where the saddle had rubbed him bald. These were the things that drove him every day. These were problems that he could solve with a simple piece of rope or a sharp knife or a keen effort.

Ma's troubles were something else. The baby could be sick, or the creditors pressing for repayment of the money Ma had had to borrow to buy seed and hire extra hands. The barn might need fixing, or the crops could be failing. There could be a whole slew of things. Once Bill knew about them, they would become his problems. Problems he would be helpless to solve.

And once he'd gotten and read a letter from his family, he was as good as obliged to write them back. Failing to do so would cause worry, or at the least hurt feelings. What was he supposed to tell them? That he was having a good time? That the job was everything he'd dreamed of, that he belonged on the freight train, that he did not want to return home? Bill knew that it wasn't right for him to be enjoying himself. Not after what had happened. Not after Ma was struggling to keep the farm running without going broke.

The little group had broken up. Ferd was already gone. Hank started to follow him, then looked back at Bill.

"Ain't you coming?"

"Sure I am," Bill said. "I'm just gonna rest a spell longer. I know as soon as I get moving, somebody'll spot me and give me a job to do."

"Speaking of jobs, you washed my clothes yet?" Hank asked rather sharply.

"Your clothes?" Bill asked. "I didn't know . . . I mean, nobody asked me . . . it ain't a problem, I just—"

Hank gave a little hoot.

"Darn it, boy, you sure are easy to fool." Hank walked away, happily talking to himself about clothes washing and tenderfeet.

Bill sat down on the grass and drew his knees

up to his chin. He looked around at the people and animals milling about the fort. They all seemed to have something to do, or looked as if they were on their way to somewhere important. Bill realized he didn't even know where the postmaster was, or where the mail was kept.

Wild Bill Hickok was striding through the parade, his long lean legs taking the distance in easy steps. Every so often a group of men would pause and watch him as he passed. Then they would put their heads together and murmur. Bill could imagine what they were saying. There's the fella who put ten shots through a knothole in a tree while galloping by. Shot the hat clear off the head of a man who'd sassed him. Always shot from the hip, and never, never missed.

He seemed to be headed straight for Bill. Even from forty paces or so, Bill could see the piercing blue of Hickok's sad eyes as they met his own. The sadness was set off by a wry smile curling up from beneath the marksman's well-tended mustache. No one knew how Wild Bill Hickok managed to look so dapper all the time, when most of the bullwhackers wore the same ratty work clothes and sweat-drooped hats every day. His brown hair was always neatly parted in the middle and combed behind his ears, where it tumbled in an elegant fashion to his shoulders. His mustache was smooth and soft, each side curling in perfect conformity to the other. Hank

Bassett said that Wild Bill sometimes wore a small, neatly trimmed goatee beard. But on this trip his chin was smoothly shaven, jutting forward from his face like a dare.

Bill got to his feet as Hickok approached. It seemed the respectful thing to do.

"Got something for ya," Hickok said, handing two envelopes to Bill.

"Thank you, James," Bill replied. He didn't look at the envelopes—he didn't have to. He knew as well as Wild Bill did what they were.

"Postmaster here is a friend a mine," Hickok said. "You get your letter to me tonight, and I'll make sure it gets into his hand and goes out on the first stage south."

"Thank you," Bill said again. No matter Bill's feelings on the subject of letter writing, Wild Bill Hickok had made it clear he expected Bill to read the mail and respond before nightfall. Though part of Bill felt indignant that Wild Bill should make it his business to see he wrote to his ma, it was also a relief to have the decision out of his hands. Nobody crossed Wild Bill Hickok. And if Wild Bill Hickok wanted a person to write a letter, well then that's exactly what he did.

Bill found a quiet spot just inside the mess hall, which was mostly deserted at this late afternoon hour. There were two letters, one from Ma and one from Julia. Bill opened Ma's.

July 20, 1857

Dear Bill,

I think of you so many times each day, but it seems there is never a moment to write you a proper letter. Little Charlie has gone to sleep early tonight, and I hope he will stay quiet long enough for me to finish this. He is never still for long, Bill! I don't remember you being that way at two years. Just this morning, when we all had our backs turned no longer than a minute, he opened the cabin door and dashed off. I'm sure you can imagine we were quite sick with worry, all running in different directions and calling his name. It was Julia who found him, and Bill, you cannot think where he was! In the cow pasture, lying on his stomach, with his face pressed right against the snout of that old bull you named Thunder! I scarcely took a breath while Julia walked very slowly and quietly to them, picked Charlie up, and handed him over the fence to me. We all scolded Charlie dreadfully, telling him he might have been gored or stepped on, but he would have none of it. Charlie thinks that Thunder is his friend, and he won't listen to anyone who says otherwise. Sometimes I think we ought to build a special pen and keep Charlie safely inside it!

Eliza Alice has finished her quilt. You remember it, Bill, as she began it before you left as a gift for your former teacher, Miss Lyons. The quilt is absolutely lovely. Eliza's stitches are the smallest and neatest I've ever seen.

Mary Hannah has learned to churn butter, and she is so enthusiastic about it that we now have more butter and buttermilk than we can use. Fortunately the hired men can always be counted on to want the extra. Nellie has really taken to riding, although I feel she might better use her spare time to improve her sewing skills. I do allow her to take Prince out every now and again, as I know he is a horse to be trusted, and I do hope you do not mind this, Bill, especially as the animal needs his exercise.

Julia will be returning to Leavenworth in September to take some more schooling. She will board with the family of her friend Marcy Delahay. I hate to have her gone, but this can be an advantage in her education, and I am willing to endure her absence.

The most exciting news I have to tell you, Bill, is that Martha has been seeing a great deal of her young man, John Crane. And now they are to be married! They have fixed a date for February. We are already busy making plans, and Eliza Alice says she wants to sew the wedding dress herself! I don't know what but she might be able to do it.

Now I need to speak seriously, Bill. I am concerned about the rough influences I am sure you are exposed to each day. I trust that you will close your ears to the profane language I am certain is being used in your presence. Please remember your upbringing at all times, and endeavor to conduct yourself as a Cody, regardless of how those around you may behave. Are you remembering to wash your face and teeth each morning and night? Are you keeping your hat and clothes clean, and using the comb I packed for you? Last of all, Bill, though I know you are required to follow orders, I fervently hope that you are remembering that Sunday belongs to the Lord, and that you are remembering to say your prayers.

I hope that you will have time to send us a letter, Bill. We are all missing you. Until you come home, please make sure you are getting enough to eat.

With love and blessings,
Ma

Bill laughed out loud. Ma's worries and reminders could be a heavy burden to bear at home, but from a distance they delighted him. Oh, what she must be imagining! Bill fashioned a picture of himself in Ma's mind, grimy faced and greasy haired, with brown hands and black fingernails and yellow teeth, chewing tobacco and spitting, and periodically shouting "goddamn me!" And he had not needed to worry that she would bring up unwelcome subjects.

Bill wrote back a short but neat letter, thanking her for the news and telling her that she would be proud to know most of the folks in his outfit. He omitted any mention of Wild Bill Hickok, as he suspected she might not find his presence as appealing as Bill did. He did stress that, like all Majors & Russell outfits, the trains were prohibited from traveling on Sundays, and the wagon master, Lew Simpson, made sure that the Sabbath was observed each week. He also told her that the wagoner's oath he'd signed prohibited him and all other bullwhackers from the use of any profanity, though Bill did not add that this restriction was enforced only in the presence of George Woods or Mr. Simpson. The more Ma approved of Majors & Russell, the better. Though he did not mention it in his letter, Bill was already planning to stay on with the bull outfit as long as they'd have him. A teamster's life was the life for him.

He held Julia's letter in his hand without opening it. Bill knew Julia's letter was much more likely to present the truth of how the family was doing in Bill's absence. She would tell him if Ma was sick, when Ma had not mentioned her own health at all. She would tell him if they had enough to eat, and if they were managing to pay for supplies. She is probably miserable, Bill thought. What if she begs me to come home?

Bill looked at the envelope for another moment, then folded it and tucked it into his pocket.

There were some things, he decided, it was simply better not to know.

Not yet.

Chapter Six
THE EMIGRANT TRAIN

★   ★   ★

Ash Hollow was a popular camping spot, not the least because of the spring of clear, cold water there, a welcome change from the murky river water of the Platte, which was the men's usual drink. When Bill's outfit arrived, there were already two groups of emigrants making camp for the evening. Though Mr. Simpson usually liked to camp apart from emigrants, he decided they should camp alongside the others. Being close to all that

fresh water made up for having to rub elbows with strangers.

It had been an exhausting approach. Ash Hollow lay at the end of a steep ravine descent, and it had required the use of the drag brakes, lock chains, and the brute strength of men and oxen to coax the wagons down the slope without allowing them to career out of control. It was little wonder after such difficult labor that most outfits chose to rest up at the Hollow.

Having arrived at last, Bill found it well worth the effort. The place grew wild with flowers and currant bushes, and the first trees that Bill had seen for days. And he could not get enough of the cool, clean water from the spring. He took frequent drinks of his own as he collected bucketful after bucketful and delivered it to thirsty teamsters. But for all the beauty of Ash Hollow, the place also contained grim reminders of what the trail to Oregon held for some. It was dotted with makeshift graves, some marked with simple piles of rocks and others with carved wooden boards or old wagon wheels with names and dates burned into them. Bill had seen graves on the trail before, but he had not spent time camping among them, where they were a constant sobering presence.

The two groups of emigrants, who all together had more than thirty wagons, were a lively set. The camp was filled with new and unfamiliar sounds. As

Bill set to work gathering wood and buffalo chips for the supper cookfire, he tried to separate the noises and identify them. He had almost forgotten what a crying baby sounded like, or the giggling of girls, or the singing of working women. They were the sounds of home, he thought, but multiplied tenfold.

Bending over to scoop up several dry, patty-shaped chips, he was startled to hear a voice behind him.

"I tell you he's an Indian," said the voice.

Bill turned around to face two girls. One looked to be about Julia's age, maybe fourteen. The other could have been nine or ten—it was difficult to say. They were both nicely dressed, considering their travels, and had brown hair and clean faces. Bill guessed at once they must be sisters.

"That's no Indian," said the older girl. "He just needs to wash his face, you'll see."

"Well, he looks downright wild," said the younger girl.

Bill was irritated to have this discussion going on as if he were not there at all.

"I ain't wild," he said, defensively. "I'm from Kansas."

The sisters burst into laughter, making Bill even more irritated.

"Girls," he said, shaking his head in disgust. "Some things are the same no matter where a man goes."

He began walking away. Undeterred, they followed him.

"No matter where a *man* goes? Do you see a *man* anywhere, Adrietta?" asked the elder sister.

"No, Celia," the younger girl replied. "Only one wild boy."

Bill turned around and gave the sisters a grim look.

"I am not a wild boy," he said.

"Buffalo boy, then," said Celia, nodding daintily at Bill's chip bucket.

"Name's Bill, if you must know," he said.

"Buffalo Bill," Celia said, and Adrietta giggled.

"Just Bill," he said firmly.

"Just Bill," repeated Celia.

Bill didn't know why he didn't just keep walking away from the pair, with their ridiculously well-combed hair and their mocking ways. It wasn't as if he enjoyed being made fun of. But something in the teasing manner of the two girls reminded him of his sisters, especially Julia and Nellie.

"We've come from Iowa," said the one called Adrietta.

"I used to be from Iowa," Bill said. "I mean, I lived in Iowa before Kansas Territory."

"Muscatine," said Celia.

"LeClaire," said Bill, pleasantly surprised. "We would have been neighbors, practically."

"We're going to Oregon," said Adrietta eagerly. "Pa says it's the land of milk and honey, and we're going to get rich!"

"Hush, Adrietta," said Celia, scowling.

"What? I only said—"

Celia silenced her sister with a pointy-toed nudge. The sight of her little foot unaccountably brought a blush to Bill's cheeks. Suddenly he was acutely aware that he hadn't bathed in weeks, his clothes were covered in mud and dust, and he was holding a bucket of buffalo chips in front of himself. Abruptly, he took a few steps backward.

"I have to do my chores," he said.

"Fine then," said Celia, a bit huffily.

"I'm with the bull outfit," Bill added hastily. But of course he was, that would be obvious. He tried again. "I work for wages. The fellas count on me to do my part."

"Do they beat you if you're lazy?" Adrietta asked. That sounded to Bill like something Nellie would say.

"Land's sake, Adrietta, the things you say," Celia said. "We'll let you get on with your chores," she added.

"Can't start the cook fire till I bring these in," Bill explained further, then almost kicked himself for bringing attention to the buffalo chips again.

Celia took Adrietta by the hand.

"Come on, Adrietta," she said. She started to lead

her sister away, then called over her shoulder, "We're the McIntires—come have supper with us if you like."

Bill couldn't think of a polite way to say no, so he said nothing as Celia and Adrietta skipped back in the direction of the encampment. Then he got to thinking about it. Between Ma's letter and the girls' resemblance to his own sisters, he was beginning to miss home. Certain things about home, that was. Such as Ma's cooking. Such as eating something other than bacon and beans for dinner. Such as talking to folks close to his own age. Now he was glad he hadn't said no. But he hadn't said yes, either. Would they be expecting him? Should he have said something either way?

But there was no time to waste working out what he should have said. He had to finish collecting fuel for the fire so he could find himself a comb and a bar of soap.

"I already said I don't need nuthin' else," Green said to Bill in his brisk way.

"What do you keep pestering Green for?" asked Hiram. "And why ain't you having any grub?"

"He looks sick," Hank said. "Are you ailing, Bill? Come here."

Bill stood where he was, so Hank came over and examined him with elaborate seriousness, checking his face, the back of his neck, and his arms and legs, and holding his hand to Bill's forehead.

"Oh my goodness," Hank said, stepping back from Bill suddenly. "Boys, this is bad."

"What's ailing him?" asked Hiram. Hank was looking truly alarmed, and even Bill began to get nervous.

"Oh dear," Hank said, sounding flustered. "I only seen this once before in all my life. I ain't sure there's any cure for it."

Bill pressed his hands to his stomach. What had Hank seen? Could it be cholera?

"Well, spit it out, Hank, what's the boy got?" Hiram asked.

"I am afraid that our extra hand has come down with a very serious case of . . . clean."

"Clean?" asked Bill. Was this a new disease he'd never heard of?

"That's right," said Hank, solemnly. "Boys, I'm sorry to have to be the one to break it to you, as I know some of you were getting right fond of the pup. But this boy has been washed clean!"

Green shook his head in an irritated way and went back to work. He was never amused by Hank's jokes, nor was he very interested in anything to do with Bill.

"Clean?" asked Ferd. "I don't believe it! Let me see!"

Bill began to squirm away from Hank, who was

holding on to him by one of his elbows.

"Why, it's true, the boy's as clean as a whistle!" Ferd exclaimed. "Just look at them ears, pink as piglets!"

"Well, don't bring him over here—it might be catchin'," said Hiram, putting his hands out in front of him in a mock gesture of self-defense.

"What's come over you, son?" Ferd asked.

"Maybe he got jumped by a couple bars of lye soap," said Hank. "They're sneaky, them soap bars. Got jumped by one myself once, but I never let it happen again."

"Maybe he's met a gal over in the emigrants' outfit," Hiram said. Bill turned red and scowled. Why wouldn't Hiram just be quiet?

"'S that right? Have you found a sweetheart, Bill?" Hiram repeated.

"Oh, let him alone, Hiram," said Hank, suddenly. "Is Bill all done with his chores, Green?"

"I done said so three times now. You're all starting to act like pups," Green muttered.

"Well then, Bill, if you got somewhere you want to be, nobody's stopping you," Hank said kindly, letting go his hold of Bill.

Bill left as fast as he could without running.

Dozens of small fires dotted the camp. Bill wandered for a few minutes, then stopped and asked a woman standing over a pot of stew where he might find the McIntires' wagon. She pointed out the spot, just a few wagons away. As he walked toward it, he could hear the sound of Adrietta's giggle. Suddenly he felt shy. Maybe Celia was only being polite asking him to supper. Why had he supposed she meant it? She had probably forgotten about it the second she lost sight of him. He should just go back to his own outfit, where he belonged. But then he heard Celia's voice right behind him.

"Why, Bill, have you come for supper?"

Bill turned around and almost jumped, Celia was standing so close to him.

"I didn't mean to scare you," Celia said, taking a step back.

"You didn't scare me," Bill replied, making himself laugh to prove it. "I was just looking for your family's wagon."

"It's right over there," Celia said. "We'll be eating soon. You have come for supper, haven't you?"

Bill nodded, feeling suddenly that his pants were too short and his hat too frayed to have supper with anyone but the bullwhackers. Then he remembered he hadn't worn his hat.

"Come walk with me once around the camp," Celia said. "We've just time."

Bill was curious about the other emigrants, and eager to see new faces after weeks of traveling with the same men.

"All right," he said. He felt a little awkward, and wasn't quite sure what to do with his hands. Finally he thrust them into his pockets.

"Over there is the Buchanans' wagon," Celia said, nodding to the left. "Three sets of twins, Mrs. Buchanan has, and the youngest still nursing. Plus two more boys and a girl. They could make their own bull outfit one day!"

Bill laughed. He could hear lots of noise from the direction of the Buchanans' wagon—crying, laughter, singing.

"How many in your family, Bill?" Celia asked.

"Five sisters and one little brother," he replied.

"Six little ones sounds like the perfect-sized family," Celia stated, ignoring the fact that including Bill, the children in his family numbered seven. "I shall have six children, three boys and three girls. Why did they let you leave?" she asked suddenly.

"Let me leave?" Bill asked. He thought she might mean the bull outfit. As the two of them rounded the far corner of the encampment, Bill could hear the sound of raised voices, male and female.

"The Burnses," Celia said, gesturing in the direction of the argument. "Always fighting, night and day. Why did your folks let you leave, I meant. They don't mind you working the bull outfit and being away from them so long?"

"It's a help to Ma, actually," Bill said. He hoped

enough had been said on the subject, but Celia continued.

"What about your pa? Doesn't he want you to stay home at least till your little brother has grown some?"

Bill took a long breath. Thinking about something that made him mad wasn't going to work in this situation. He remained silent for a moment. Then he thought, She's only a girl, after all. Like Julia. It doesn't count, telling a girl.

"My pa died," Bill said. His voice sounded small and sad, and having heard himself say the words, he immediately regretted it.

Celia stopped walking and faced Bill, her face serious.

"When?" she asked.

"About four months ago," Bill said. "He took sick," he added after a moment.

"Oh, Bill, how dreadful." Celia reached out suddenly and squeezed Bill's hand. Bill had been looking away, but when he turned and looked at her, he was surprised to see tears of sympathy welling in her eyes. Please, don't let her start me crying, Bill pleaded silently.

But Celia seemed to understand that enough had been said. She pulled on Bill's hand, and once he was walking beside her, she let it go. They walked in silence for a few moments, approaching a battered wagon whose cover had been badly patched many times.

"Whose is that?" Bill asked, and Celia laughed.

"The Walker brothers," Celia said. "They've the worst luck of any men alive. They've broken wagon wheels, been overturned while crossing a stream, and sunk in the mud three times. And one of their mules was killed by lightning, and they had to lighten their load by throwing half their things out of the wagon!"

"And they haven't given up?" Bill said.

"Nothing to go back to," Celia said. "They came over on the boat from Scotland. Many of these folks did. My ma and pa both came here from Scotland too, before they were married. Some of these folks are distant kin," she added with a rueful smile. "Though I'm not sure I care to find out which ones, if you know what I mean."

Bill laughed. They had come almost full circle now, and he could see Adrietta standing in front of the McIntires' wagon. When she caught sight of Bill and Celia, she stamped one foot and pursed her lips.

"Where did you go? Why didn't you take me? Why doesn't anyone ever take me anywhere?" Adrietta demanded.

"We're taking you to Oregon, aren't we?" Celia said, reaching out and rubbing her sister's head affectionately as they passed her. "Here's my folks," she said to Bill.

Celia led him past her wagon to a campfire, where an auburn-haired woman was sitting on a log with a baby on her lap.

"Ma, this is Bill, the boy from the bull outfit I told you about."

Mrs. McIntire smiled warmly at Bill.

"Welcome, Bill. We're pleased to have you for supper." She spoke with a pleasant burr, unlike anything Bill had heard before.

"Thank you, ma'am," Bill replied.

He might have picked Mrs. McIntire out of the entire camp, she so closely resembled her two daughters. She had an oval-shaped face and fine, wavy hair pulled back in a bun. Though she had tired circles under her eyes, her expression was merry all the same. Mr. McIntire, who had been watering his team, came over to the fire now and gave Bill a friendly nod. He was a bluff, broad man with a long beard and thinning red hair. Bill introduced himself, though Mr. McIntire already seemed to know who he was, and the two shook hands. Bill was happy to see that both Celia's parents seemed cheerful and kind, and he began to feel more comfortable.

Celia tended the stew, stirring the pot that was suspended on a spit over the fire. In the flickering firelight her face seemed to change—one minute she looked older, and the next younger. She glanced up at Bill, and he quickly looked down at his shoes.

"Bill's a bullwhacker, but they don't beat him,"

Adrietta announced. "At least, that's what he says."

"You're with one of Majors and Russell's outfits, isn't it?" said Mr. McIntire.

Bill nodded.

"That's hard work," Mr. McIntire said. "You must be a good worker."

"I guess I am. I'm only the extra hand, not a bull-whacker," Bill said. "But it's hard work. I do like it, though."

"I can imagine I'd have liked such work as a lad," said Mr. McIntire. His burr was much thicker than his wife's.

Celia had begun to serve bowls of stew. She gave Bill his first, but he made sure to wait until everyone had one before he began eating.

"Celia says you came over from Scotland," Bill said, because ma always told him it was polite to show you were interested in other folks when you talked to them.

"We certainly did, by the grace of God," said Mr. McIntire.

"By the grace of God indeed," added Mrs. McIntire, reaching over and laying her hand on her husband's arm.

"Tell the story, Pa," said Celia. Adrietta chimed in immediately.

"Yes, Pa, tell the story!"

Mr. McIntire obviously didn't mind, because he smiled and leaned his back against the log where his wife was sitting, getting into a comfortable position.

"The McIntires and the Blacks, that's Mrs. McIntire's family, had been friends for generations. Like one family, we were. And when it was decided that the four eldest from each family should go to America, we were made brave by the thought of going together. I was sixteen, and I didn't have much. But I remember we all argued about having to fit everything into one trunk, and Elizabeth and her three brothers were to fit all of their things into another. How we battled with each other about what could be brought along, who could bring this book, that extra dress. In the end we almost didn't go at all, so desperately we wrangled about our possessions. But somehow we sorted it out and booked passage on a sailing ship. Bill, it was the loveliest vessel you can imagine. Three great masts and a swooping, high prow. It seemed to have come from heaven itself. But once our journey began, we began to feel the ship was more cursed than blessed."

"Why?" Bill asked.

"Bad things happened every week," Mr. McIntire said. "It was almost more than a person could believe. Sickness came over the passengers, and four died the first week, with many more seriously weakened. Two girls were swept over the side in rough seas. A sailor fell from the rigging and broke his neck. A rivalry broke out over a young woman, and one man was killed and another gravely wounded. And an old man, a member of the crew, began telling strange stories of a sea serpent, which he said was following our ship."

"Did you see it?" Bill asked, his eyes wide. Mr. McIntire shook his head.

"That I did not," he said. "But the stories alone gave Elizabeth nightmares, and more than one of us secretly feared for our lives. It was a two-month journey across the ocean, Bill, and little did we know the worst of our luck was saved for the very last. We were close enough to see the coast, but a powerful gale had blown up and was sweeping us toward the rocks. Try as he might, there was nothing our captain could do, and just after midnight we struck those rocks and foundered.

"We had all been ordered below, and the eight of us, four McIntires and four Blacks, sat holding each other's hands and praying. We prayed with all our might that each of us would be delivered from that storm without harm. And the next morning, when the gale had blown itself out, we found we were still alive. The ship itself was beyond repair, but the captain had fired his musket to signal for help, and that help did come. Several small rowboats began ferrying passengers ashore, and one came for us, but there was no room for our trunks. And that is how we came to America, Bill, wet and bruised and frightened, with not a possession to our name but the soggy clothes on our backs."

"But we were together," Mrs. McIntire added.

"Aye," said Mr. McIntire. "And together still, aren't we?"

Bill looked back and forth between them, trying to imagine them struggling from a sinking ship.

"And was there really a curse? Was there really a sea monster?" Bill asked.

Mr. McIntire gave Bill a thoughtful look, then his lips curled into a tiny smile.

"Oh, I don't expect so. But I suppose we will never truly know," he said softly.

Celia turned to Bill.

"Isn't that a wonderful story?" she asked. Bill had to agree that it was. In fact, he'd been so entranced by visions of the cursed ship trailed by a sea serpent that he was surprised to find the sun had set completely, and it was almost dark. The new moon and a handful of stars were already visible.

"Did you get enough stew, Bill?" Celia asked.

"Oh yes, thank you," Bill replied. Celia really was awfully nice, he thought.

"Once Celia let the pot fall into the fire," said Adrietta. "And we had to beg bread and salt pork for supper from the Dickersons."

"Hush, Adrietta," said Celia, looking at Bill to see how he was reacting to this news of her disgrace. "It wasn't my fault and you know it."

"Well, you were the one tending it," Adrietta countered, and the two girls began a lively debate over the facts.

The sound of Celia's and Adrietta's voices as they interrupted each other reminded him of home. He felt happy and comfortable. Strains of music floated into the air.

"Dickerson has his fiddle out tonight," Mr. McIntire said.

"Look, some folks are dancing," Celia cried. "Ma, may we go and watch?"

"I don't know that Bill will be interested in watching people dance, Celia," Mrs. McIntire said.

"Oh, I am," Bill said. "I mean, I don't mind. We don't get much music in the bull outfit."

"May we go, Ma?" wheedled Adrietta. When Mrs. McIntire nodded, Adrietta squealed and clapped her hands.

"Come on!" she said, stomping a foot. "We'll miss it if you don't hurry!"

Celia stuck her tongue out at Adrietta when her mother wasn't looking, then followed her sister toward the sound of the fiddling, pausing to let Bill walk beside her. There were eight or ten couples dancing a reel, and others gathered around, tapping their feet and clapping. Bill and the girls found a comfortable place to settle. Adrietta sat on one side of Bill and Celia on the other.

It was a wonderful night. Being around so many

families, hearing music and laughter, and feeling full after a satisfying stew and a good story all put Bill in mind of home. And yet he had never been farther away from his home in all his life.

Bill sneaked a look at Celia. She had a delighted smile on her face, and her eyes eagerly watched the dancers as they swung about. Bill would not have minded sitting there all night, listening to the merry scratch of the fiddle and watching folks celebrate under the vast Nebraska sky. They all seemed to be having so much fun, and Bill was happy just to sit by and drink it all in.

Mr. Simpson had the outfit underway by dawn. The emigrants were still having their breakfast and gathering their teams when the bullwhackers rolled out. Bill had said his good-byes last night, but nonetheless he tried to catch a glimpse of the McIntires. In the dim morning light he could not pick their wagon out from the others.

The bull train moved quickly, and the two emigrant trains would not overtake them. Like so many thousands of other families, the McIntires would continue their quest to reach the west coast, and more likely than not Bill would never know what became of Celia and her Scottish kin.

But he would not forget their story.

CHAPTER SEVEN

STAMPEDE

★   ★   ★

Drinking on the job was strictly prohibited, and with good reason. The long hours of driving in the dusty wheel ruts of the wagon ahead could get mind-numbingly boring. But a man never knew when he might have to spring into action at a moment's notice. It was crucial to stay alert. The monotonous plodding could turn into a dangerous situation at any time.

Everyone knew who broke what rules, and

like the others in the outfit, Bill had a pretty good idea who the secret drinkers were. But he never said anything. In this way the teamsters were like brothers. You didn't rat on another fella, and he wouldn't rat on you. As long as a man was doing his job, and not putting his animals or anyone else's in harm's way, his secret was safe with the other bullwhackers.

Bill knew that as far as drinking went, Clayton Ewell was far and away the worst offender. Riding Mike up and down the line, Bill had often noticed Ewell stumbling unevenly beside his team. And though almost all bullwhackers drove their wagons while walking on the left side of their oxen, Ewell frequently rode perched on the front of his wagon. Of course, most bullwhackers sat a spell every now and again. But Ewell would just stay there. There were times, passing him by, that Bill could swear the man was fast asleep.

On this particular afternoon Bill was absorbed by the sight of Chimney Rock in the distance, shimmering like a snake about to strike in the full heat of the day. Bill could not have dreamed up such a sight if he'd tried. It was a massive pyramid of rock and grass, topped by a pillar of wind-worn rock that looked to Bill like a giant hand pointing up to the sky. He guessed it might be five hundred feet high. The sight of it made Bill want to run to its base and start climbing. But Green assured Bill that the rock was a good many miles farther away than it looked.

Riding up the line for the twentieth time that day, Bill's gaze was still firmly on Chimney Rock when he heard the first telltale rumbles of thunder. He scanned the sky from horizon to horizon, but he could not pick out a single cloud in the ocean of blue. Confused, he slowed Mike up, and a glance to his right showed him a team trudging along of its own accord, as Clayton Ewell slumped, hat pulled down over his eyes, up on the front edge of the wagon, his feet propped up by the chain connecting the wagon to the yokes.

The thunder was growing louder, in a long unceasing sound. Up and down the line Bill began to hear the shouts of men. He looked in the direction of the Platte River, and when he saw a cloud of dust swirling and dancing toward the train, he understood with a sickening lurch in his stomach. This was no thunderstorm. It was a herd of buffalo on the stampede, and they were making straight for the train.

There was no time to get out of the way. A team of eight oxen pulling a heavy load could not simply veer to the side and rush off the road without tipping over the wagon. Through the dust storm raised by the pounding hooves, Bill could see the giant forms of the buffalo. He guessed there were at least five hundred of them. The train of twenty-five wagons had spread out over a mile as they traveled across the plains. Those at the head of the line might get themselves clear, but those back near the rear were going to see the bulk of the buffalo rush right into them.

On his wagon close to the rear of the train, Clayton Ewell dozed, oblivious to the approaching catastrophe. Bill rode alongside and shouted his name, but his shouts fell on deaf ears. If the rumble of five hundred stampeding buffalo did not wake Clayton Ewell, Bill's voice certainly wasn't going to either. Bill hesitated only for a moment. If he got onto the wagon beside Ewell, Mike was going to be on his own. Bill would not be able to help him escape the stampede. But the choice was between a mule and a man, and though Bill would have chosen Mike over Ewell as a bunkmate any day, this was a life-threatening situation.

Swiftly tying off the reins to the saddle so Mike would not trip over them, Bill dismounted and gave Mike a hard slap on the rear. He shouted "Git, Mike!" To his relief, Mike turned and veered away from the stampeding herd. Then Bill clambered up onto the wagon and squeezed himself behind Ewell. There was barely room for both of them.

"Clayton Ewell! Clayton!" Bill yelled, pummeling on the man's arm. Ewell stirred slightly. But it was too late. Suddenly they were inside the cloud of dirt and the herd was upon them. The cloud swallowed them up like a mudhole, sucking them into the midst of the charging animals. Panicked, the ox team ran forward as fast as it could go, switching direction frequently.

Bill pressed his back against the wagon's canvas cover to brace himself, and wrapped his legs around Ewell, as if they were two boys sledding. The noise had become a roar. Bill was aware of a hoof here, a horn there, little glimpses of fur and blue sky. The wagon jerked and lurched. Had Bill not been holding Clayton Ewell, the bullwhacker would have been knocked off the wagon and under the hooves of the buffalo. Bill felt sick and disoriented, and finally he squeezed his eyes shut and just held on to Ewell for dear life. Bill had no idea how long the stampede went on. It felt like fifteen minutes, but could have been three. But eventually the sound began to fade, and Ewell's team slowed down and stopped of their own accord. Bill opened his eyes and looked around.

The team and wagon had been turned completely around. Bill heard a bellow and could see that some of Ewell's team had become snagged in their gear. The orderly wagon train was gone. Some of the teams were running wild, dragging their wagons and bull-whackers off in any direction. Several teams had gotten loose, and Bill could see two wagons that had turned over.

Bill jumped off the wagon and began calming the frightened team by saying their names and patting them. Fortunately, Ewell's oxen were a particularly docile group, and though their eyes were wide and their breath coming in startled snorts, they stood still as Bill began to disentangle them from their gear.

Clayton Ewell was fully awake now. He rubbed his eyes and scratched at the back of his neck while looking around him in bleary confusion.

"Buffalo stampede," Bill said, coaxing an ox's leg off the chain holding the team together.

"I can see that," Ewell said, his voice thick and harsh. He jumped to the ground, took a few faltering steps, and made a shooing gesture as if waving away a swarm of mosquitoes.

"Get out of my hair and let me see to my damn team," Ewell barked.

"I already seen to them," Bill replied hotly.

"Are you deaf? I said get out of my hair!" Ewell repeated.

Bill shrugged. There were plenty of other places he was needed. He walked toward the next team, looking all the while for Mike. His face was calm, but under his collar his neck burned hot with anger.

It took the rest of that day and all of the following one to repair the damage done by the stampede. Fortunately, none of the men had been seriously injured, but four oxen had been killed, and over a dozen were missing. Several of the wagons had had the pivots and chains snapped clear off, and most had at least one wheel that needed fixing. Mike had trotted back into camp of his own accord, his saddle askew but otherwise none the worse for wear. Bill was filled with relief and affection for the homely animal, and managed to sneak him an apple.

At noon on the second day the familiar cook's song rang out, a welcome sound to the tired men. As Bill's mess gathered, he came face-to-face with Clayton Ewell for the first time since the stampede. Bill said nothing to the bullwhacker, though he noticed the man looked weak and his face had taken on a sickly pallor.

As he headed for his mess, Bill caught sight of Wild Bill Hickok, standing to one side of his team with his hat in his hands. He was staring out across the plains. Bill paused as he approached him. Wild Bill seemed lost in thought, and Bill almost didn't speak. But at the last minute he did.

"Would you care to join my mess for some grub, James? I'm on bread duty," Bill said. Wild Bill didn't keep to any one mess, as the other men did. He simply ate where he pleased.

Bill stood for a moment, waiting for an answer. But James remained silent. He had glanced at Bill when he approached, but now he stood with his back to the boy, still staring.

"James?" Bill repeated again after a moment. Wild

Bill whirled suddenly around.

"Dammit, leave me be!" Wild Bill snapped.

Bill took a step back, stunned. Trying to swallow his hurt, Bill muttered "sorry" and walked over to Green's fire, where the mess was gathering. He began gathering the ingredients for the bread, aware that Hank was watching him. He pretended not to notice, but Hank walked over.

"Don't mind when Hickok gets in one of his tempers, Bill," Hank said quietly. "Happens to him from time to time, and when it does he'd bark at his own ma."

Bill nodded, trying not to look as if he cared, though Hank's words helped his hurt feelings to subside. He glanced around, wondering who else had seen Wild Bill snub him.

"Now Bill," said Hank a little louder. "Last time you made bread, I found the rattle from an old snake in my slice. And the time afore that, there was a bug as big as my thumb. I keep telling you, you got to be more careful what you let in that bowl!"

Bill laughed and turned his attention to the bread. Though you wouldn't know to hear Hank tell it, Bill had actually become rather accomplished at his baking, and could now produce a golden loaf cooked thoroughly through. He set the dough in the dutch oven and placed it over the coals. When it was done, he served the bread up to the bullwhackers. Though tired, the men were generally in good humor. The stampede had created hours of work, but it was also a change from their routine and gave them something to talk about.

"George Woods said a buffalo got himself tangled in Steve Carp's wagon chain and broke the thing clear in half trying to get free," Ferd Smith was saying with his mouth full.

"That's nothing," said Hank, filling his cup with water from the bucket. "I myself saw a buffalo running off to the north with a whole yoke hanging off one of his horns."

Several snorts of disbelief erupted from the circle.

"Hank Bassett, I don't believe you ever met a tall tale you didn't take to," said Hiram, taking a long sip of water and pouring what was left in his cup over the top of his dusty head.

"That just shows what you know," said Hank. "I know a thing or two about stampedes."

"And I guess we're also supposed to believe that story you been telling about yourself since the beginning of time?" asked Ferd.

"Well, why wouldn't you?" Hank asked. "Every word of it's true. But look how rude I'm being. I don't believe young Bill knows this story."

There was a chorus of groans.

"Don't you dare tell that old story again," yelled Hiram. "My poor ears will not have it."

"I'd like to hear it," Bill said suddenly, and Hank gave him an enormous smile and clapped him on the back.

"*Bill* would like to hear it," Hank said triumphantly. Another series of groans rang out, but no one moved.

"Now Bill, I reckon I was just a little older than you at the time," Hank began. "I was riding with a wagon train of emigrants crossing the plains, not far from this very spot. Hired myself out to them, I had, as a scout."

"Errand boy's more like it," Ferd said. Hank ignored him.

"We were cresting a hill when we saw a party of hunters crossing a river ahead. They must have spooked a herd of buffalo grazing nearby, because the herd began to run off in our direction. Several of the fools began to chase down the buffalo, which only made the herd run at us faster. Well, those emigrants weren't all that experienced with mules, which is what they had pulling their wagons. Mules scare easier than oxen, and they began to panic like a bunch of baby squirrels. They were going in every direction, running wild and getting tangled up in other teams' gear. I got separated from the train, and bit by bit those buffalo were forcing me closer and closer to the river bluff. By now I was quite a ways away from my group, and darn it, Bill, if the girth on my saddle didn't pick that very minute to snap."

Hank paused dramatically, imitating the snapping sound of breaking leather by clapping his hands.

"But fortune shone upon me, Bill, because at that moment I happened to be passing under a small tree growing on the bluff. So I reached up, grabbed a branch, and lifted myself up. My horse pitched off the saddle and sped away, and the buffalo were still stampeding underneath me. Now I was up a tree without a saddle! I had to get to the train and help those folks. So I took a breath, concentrated real hard, and dropped down onto one of the buffalo running under me. I landed solid right in the center of his back, Bill, and I got me a good handful of mane. Then I rode that bull all the way back to my train. By then the herd had stopped stampeding, and when I got where I needed to go, I jumped off nice as you please. And wouldn't you know it, by suppertime my horse had come back into camp by himself."

"Oh, get on with you, Hank," said Ferd. But Bill said he liked the story, and Hank looked pleased. Everyone continued eating, and for a long time no one spoke. Hiram wandered away to swap some tobacco with a man in another mess. Bill glanced over at Clayton Ewell. They had not had any sort of exchange since the stampede. Ewell, feeling someone looking at him, raised his head and saw Bill. His face darkened, and his expression turned to an angry sneer. Bill's insides went tight, but he kept eating. It wasn't as if he'd figured Ewell would be nice to him just because Bill had helped him out during the stampede and kept his mouth shut about it. Knowing Ewell, the entire incident would probably just make him hate Bill even more.

It was still quiet when Hiram returned and looked down where he'd left his plate. Loudly, Hiram exclaimed, "Why, some scoundrel has absquatulated with my bacon!"

The look of outrage on Hiram's face was too much for Bill, and the boy started laughing. The more he tried to stop, the harder he laughed. Then Hank produced the missing bacon, which he'd hidden in his cup, and started to laugh himself.

That night, Bill went to sleep tired and dirty, but happy.

CHAPTER EIGHT

AN ARMY OF BEARS

★　　★　　★

Wild Bill Hickok moved like a cat. He was silent and stealthy, with a powerful grace. Even when sitting, he looked ready to spring at any moment. He never announced his presence beforehand by footsteps or a hearty hello. Most times a person simply noticed that Wild Bill was among them, and how long he'd been there was anyone's guess.

Stories about him spread across the plains like a prairie fire, and there was no real way to pick the true tale from the tall tale. If half what folks said were to be believed, there was not a faster or more accurate shot in the West. He was said to be able to shoot the edge side of a dime, and with one bullet cut a chicken's neck without breaking the bone. Some claimed Wild Bill would as soon shoot you as look at you, a trait his usually gentle demeanor did not seem to support. His occasional black moods only added mystery to his reputation. He did nothing to support or deny the stories of his abilities, and his silence seemed to confirm the claims. Surely, if he didn't feel the need to brag about it, he must actually be the deadest shot alive.

No one sought Wild Bill out. He chose his friends, and he chose very few. But once he'd chosen you, he was a loyal friend. Bill did not know what he'd done to earn Wild Bill Hickok's friendship. It was a constant marvel to him. He was the youngest, shortest, and skinniest fellow in the outfit. And he was a tenderfoot. But Wild Bill saw something in him, and that was evident to everyone. And though there were always a few who remained distant or dismissive, some of the most seasoned bullwhackers were starting to call him "Wild Bill's young friend." Bill realized that the teamsters liked and appreciated any fellow who worked as hard as he did. But Bill also knew he was being accorded a respect that he might not have had without the approval of his celebrated friend.

They had come almost five hundred miles from Fort Kearny in about a month, following the Platte River until the trail went west and south away from the Platte, in the direction of the Sweetwater River. When the weather was fine and the trail smooth, it was sometimes possible for a little socializing on the move. Today happened to be one of those days, when, moving up the line, Bill fell in beside Wild Bill, and they began to talk. You never knew when Wild Bill started whether it was a real story or a fanciful one. He did love to spin a yarn.

"No, it's true," Wild Bill said, as his legs made long easy steps through the grass alongside his team. Bill was riding next to him on Mike. Wild Bill was so tall that Bill had to crane his neck to look at him if they were both walking. It was easier just to stay in the saddle and look his friend in the eye.

"I'm surprised you never heard of it," he continued.

"What did you call it?" Bill asked.

"The Underground Railroad," he replied.

"But who drives it?" Bill pressed. Wild Bill laughed.

"Isn't that kind of railroad," Wild Bill explained. "That's just what they call it. Aren't no engines, aren't no tracks. Just a silent agreement between folks who hate slavery, feel brave, and have a good hiding place on their property. Word gets out who can be trusted and who has a place. An escaping slave goes from one hiding place to the next, making his way north to the free states, or up to Canada."

"And your pa helped?" Bill asked.

"That's right. My pa had Quaker friends—now they're a whole different story. But a good many of the Quakers are friends to slaves, and they helped set the Underground Railroad up."

"Did they come to your house? How did they find you?" Bill asked.

"Word spread who to go to, who could help 'em next. My pa built two cellars in our home, but one of 'em was hidden out of sight, all lined with hay. You'd never know it was there unless somebody told you. The slaves would come in the middle of the night. It was a dangerous business. There were provost marshals out looking for 'em, and slave hunters. They captured escaped slaves and drug 'em back to their owners."

"Why would they do that?" Bill asked.

"To collect the reward. Some men'll do just about anything for money, Bill, and delivering a slave back to his owner is the least of it. A man had to be careful out there on the roads at night. Slave hunters are sneaky devils, and they'll shoot you as fast as ask your name if they think you might get in the way of their bounty."

"Did your pa ever get shot at?"

"Sure he did," Wild Bill answered. "More times'n I can count. One night me and my brother Lorenzo were along. I can't recall why. But my pa had collected two escaping slaves and hidden them in the back of his wagon under some hay. We weren't more than a mile from home when suddenly a group of three or four men jumped into the road and commenced to shooting at us!"

"What did you do?" Bill asked.

"I, sad to say, didn't do nothing at all. My pa grabbed Lorenzo and me and tossed us into the back of the wagon with the others. Then he whipped and hollered at his team for all he was worth, and they took off like a bolt of lightning. If Pa hadn't known the roads so well, those slave hunters probably would've got us. But his team was fast, and he knew all the hidden paths and lanes, and by God but if we didn't get 'em home and into that cellar without taking a single shot. That's all true, Bill, no gum."

"Your pa must have really cared about helping those slaves."

Wild Bill nodded, narrowing his eyes with the memory.

"That he did, young Bill. He had plenty of grit, my pa."

"Was that the only time you rode along with him for the Underground Railroad?" Bill asked, eager to hear more.

"Can't say as I recall," Wild Bill responded. Then a small smile played about beneath his mustache. "Course, there was the time I got cornered by a whole army of grizzly bears."

"An army of bears?"

"Sure seemed that way. Must have been five of them, anyway, some of the biggest and meanest bears you ever saw. Twelve feet high if they was an inch. Bears got good eyesight and better noses, and they knew I was there right off. And from the sounds they were making, I could see they weren't too pleased about it. Well, I had been out scouting on foot, and I noticed a kind of opening in the earth about two feet wide, running into a bluff. Now I saw right away that if I could get myself down into this opening, and shimmy myself along to the end, I'd have a wall of dirt on each side of me, as good as Fort Laramie. The way was so narrow, I figured even if the bears came in after me, they could only manage one at a time. And I'd have a fighting chance. So that's what I did. I hopped into that little space, and I hunkered down and waited to see what would happen."

Wild Bill paused then and took the opportunity to groom his mustache with careful strokes. Bill waited as patiently as possible but after several moments could not contain himself.

"Did the bears come in after you?" he asked. Wild Bill looked over at Bill, his eyes gleaming.

"Oh, that they did," Wild Bill replied. "One at a time, they came. Now I had me a six-shooter and a big knife. When that first bear came, I bided my time, then took a clean shot and killed him dead. But that just made the second bear downright ornery, and he climbed down into the hole and came at me. I took my time again and shot him. Well, that third bear followed, and so did the fourth. I took 'em both out with my last four bullets. One bear piled right on top of the next. Problem was, the biggest bear of all, looking right peevish, was fixing to climb over the pile and come give me a try himself."

Wild Bill took another pause here, this time to remove his hat and smooth his brown curls behind his ears.

"And . . . what did you do?" Bill finally asked.

"Well, Bill, all I had was my knife. And I'll admit it, I ain't quite as swift with a knife as I am with a six-shooter. So I waited till that bear was about five feet away, and I took careful aim at his heart, and I threw that knife as hard as I ever threw a thing in my life."

"And?" breathed Bill. Another buffalo stampede could be headed his way, but he wasn't moving until he heard the rest of the story.

"And," said Wild Bill, replacing his hat carefully on his head, "I missed."

"You missed?" cried Bill.

"I missed," repeated Wild Bill. "Clean miss. Knife

flew right past him, didn't so much as nick him."

There was another agonizing silence.

"Well, what happened next?" Bill cried.

Wild Bill gave Bill a long look. Then he let out a long sigh.

"Well, Bill, that bear up and killed me," said Wild Bill. And he looked straight ahead and kept walking.

Bill rode alongside him in silence. What had he missed? What had he not understood? He shot a sidelong glance at Wild Bill, who rubbed his nose and winked.

And then Bill began to laugh. And Wild Bill Hickok laughed too.

When he was done laughing, Bill asked Wild Bill why, when that last bear had him cornered, he didn't just unfold his wings and fly up into the sky. And Wild Bill laughed harder than ever, and said the next time he told that story he would end it by escaping in that very way.

More and more, Bill was learning that the West was made up of stories. Which ones were true and which ones weren't wasn't really important. What mattered was the telling, the listening, and the remembering. The truth of the stories was in their spirit.

After a time Bill heard Clayton Ewell's story. Ewell didn't tell it himself. Hank Bassett told it when Ewell wasn't around. Ewell had gone west, Hank explained to Bill, with his folks and his four sisters in '49, when the first shouts of *Gold!* had reverberated across the country. They had been headed for California with a slew of other folks, and had trouble from the start. One of Ewell's sisters had fallen off the back of the wagon and been crushed by the team behind them, who never saw her in the grass. Another of his sisters was bitten by a snake. She had suffered for two days before dying.

In the Thousand Springs Valley the train had met up with some prospectors looking for company. What they got instead was cholera, and the disease swept through the group like a summer storm. When their wagon train finally reached Sutter's Fort in California, over two thirds of the party had perished, including Ewell's remaining two sisters and both parents. Between east and west he'd lost his entire family. Folks said Ewell lost his thirst for gold then and replaced it with a thirst for whisky. He'd been drinking ever since.

The story didn't make Bill like Ewell any better. But it did quell his hatred of the man. Bill and Ewell continued to work together when they had to. They did not speak beyond the necessary exchange of information, and they took no pleasure in each other's company. But like the oxen, they were yoked together by work, and they plodded silently forward together, shoulder to shoulder.

CHAPTER NINE

TROUBLE

The weeks passed quickly, and Bill could hardly believe it was almost the end of September. When they had left Fort Leaven-worth in mid-July, the summer had been at its full power, with searing days and hot wind and thunderstorms. Now, as they crossed through the mile-long gap in the Rocky Mountains called the South Pass, the nights had gotten cold, and the outfit awoke each morning to frost-covered grass.

Mr. Simpson, the wagon master, had been a demanding but congenial boss for most of their journey. But now that they had crossed the South Pass and were less than 120 miles from Fort Bridger, he became tense and short-tempered. He ordered a meeting of the entire outfit one brisk morning, several days' travel beyond the pass.

Bill sat between Green and Hank on the ground. The wagons were still corralled in a circle from the night before, and the oxen had not yet been herded and yoked. Occasionally one bellowed. The only other sound was the crackling of the fires built at points around the circle. Bill wished he were closer to one. His toes felt frozen stiff.

Mr. Simpson stood in the center of the circle, surveying his thirty-one men.

"Boys," he said, "I expect most of you know we're just about a week's travel from Fort Bridger, if we don't get no snow."

Mr. Simpson paused to take a long drink of coffee. Bill's stomach rumbled, and he wondered for about the fiftieth time why this outfit didn't consider breakfast to be an important meal.

"Normally when we're getting close to winding things up on a trip, bullwhackers get a little lax in their duties. I ain't pointing fingers—that's just the way it's been. But this time things got to be different, and I'll tell you why."

Bill hopped up to refill Mr. Simpson's coffee. The wagon master gave him a brisk nod of thanks, and took another sip before continuing. The steam from the cup snaked around his face.

"Two reasons. First is, we left Leavenworth two

months later than most outfits. That couldn't be helped, as we didn't get the order for supplies until then. But fact is it puts us in a bad place for the cold weather. I expect you all heard stories of emigrants to Oregon getting snowbound west of Rocky Ridge. If it happened to them, it can happen to us. So we got to move fast, boys. I know Mr. Majors don't like no traveling on the Sabbath. But as wagon master, I'm suspending that rule until we reach Fort Bridger. Better to ride on a Sunday than freeze to death giving the Lord his due respect."

There were some hearty assents among the men. Bill knew many of them thought it downright foolish of the wagon master to adhere to Mr. Majors's travel rule. It was a well-known fact that the rule was ignored by other wagon masters in different outfits. For his own part, Bill enjoyed the day off, and it didn't hurt his future prospects for Ma to know he was part of such a God-fearing outfit.

"Second thing is this: We gotta keep our eyes peeled. I'm appointing a second man on guard duty every night, but during the day I'm relying on every one of you to keep a lookout."

Bill's eyes grew bigger. From everything he'd heard, there had been no problems with Indians attacking trains this summer. Had something happened to change that?

"If we come under attack, you know the procedure. If we can't outrun 'em, corral the wagons. Make sure your weapons are at the ready. But we ain't soldiers, and these ain't all our worldly possessions. It's only freight. I don't want no dead heroes, if you take my meaning."

"'Scuse me, Mr. Simpson, for acting ignorant, but who exactly are we expecting to attack? Sioux?" asked Hiram.

Bill felt thankful he hadn't asked the question when he saw the look of irritation cross the wagon master's face.

"Cummings, don't you know nothing about what we're freighting?" Simpson asked.

"Supplies?" asked Hiram, tentatively.

"What kind of supplies?" Simpson demanded.

"Army supplies?" Hiram questioned. He wasn't going to offer anything as fact at this point.

"For what army?"

Hiram Cummings looked blank, and Simpson shook his head.

"The Army of Utah, boys. General Johnston's army, what's here to deal with the Mormon rebellion."

Bill didn't know much about the religious group called the Mormons, who had traveled by the thousands from Illinois to establish a homeland in the Great Salt Lake Valley in Utah Territory. He had heard that their founder had seen angels, and that Mormon men were permitted to marry more than one wife at a time. These didn't sound like the sort of people liable to attack a bull outfit.

"There's been some bad business, and some people have been killed," Mr. Simpson continued. "Now word is the Mormons swear they'll stop the army from reaching Salt Lake City. If they aim to stop the army, you can bet they aim to stop us too. Without supplies, no army is gonna be worth much."

That made sense, anyway. Bill had a fleeting picture in his mind of a league of charging Mormons attacking the army, wives and angels bringing up the rear.

"That's all I got to say, boys, so let's pull foot and look sharp," Mr. Simpson said.

Instantly, the camp came to life as thirty-one men leapt to their feet. Bill was so accustomed to his departure chores he could do them with his eyes shut. But today he did them twice as fast while thinking hard. What was he supposed to say if he saw a Mormon? Come to think of it, how did a body tell a Mormon from a regular fellow?

The sound of several loud bullwhip cracks signaled that the first wagons in the train were underway. Bill saddled up Mike as quickly as he could with his fingers numb from the cold. Even Mike moved more slowly than usual. The mule had been a fine mount for close to two months now, and Bill had come to appreciate his strength, endurance, and loyalty. Still, he hoped no one he knew from back home ever saw him atop a mule. He'd never live it down.

The wind was relentless. During the hot weather, wind had been a mixed blessing. It cooled one's body but also carried swirls of dust, which it deposited everywhere. Bill couldn't imagine what he looked like, though he could see the dirt-dark faces of the other teamsters, growing grubbier each day. Only Wild Bill Hickok managed to stay clean. He was the only man Bill had ever heard of who valued bathing to an extraordinary degree. No matter where they camped, no matter what the weather, Wild Bill always seemed to find a watering hole in which to soap himself up and rub the grit out of his mustache. But even Wild Bill Hickok, Bill thought, was not going to bathe in this cold. Each day the temperature seemed to drop another few degrees. Bill had only a thin pair of work gloves, which were made to prevent rope burns, not keep out the cold.

And the wind had become a persistent, numbing enemy. It froze the tops of Bill's ears and the tips of his fingers. His hands felt clumsy on the reins, and his toes felt like little stones inside his boots. He found himself staring at the fur-covered oxen with a jealous eye, imagining what it would be like to travel within that covering of fur and fat. Days stretched out longer than they ever had before, though dusk came earlier each day.

It was at night that Bill experienced the true

feeling of cold for the first time. Back at the Codys' claim in Kansas Territory he had endured the winter of '55 doggedly, with a new blizzard blowing snow over the cabin every week. He remembered lying in his bed, shivering under the blankets and dreading the moment when it came time to get up and throw the covers off. Now he could only dream of the luxury of being in a bed at all, on a real hay-stuffed mattress under a wool blanket, with four walls around him and a roof over his head. Here he had only one blanket to act as mattress, pillow and covering. The cold from the frozen ground seeped straight through, making real sleep impossible.

On October 3, just after the outfit got underway, it began to snow. The sky was black-gray, and from the look of it Bill expected the snow wasn't going to let up anytime soon. The harder it snowed, the faster Lew Simpson urged them on. Midday break was cut in half. The snow had already drifted so high in some places, it was impossible for the oxen to graze. The animals couldn't be expected to pull their loads for long with no food in their stomachs. Blacksnakes cracked loudly and frequently, as the bullwhackers urged the tiring animals to hurry. Still, they were moving more and more slowly. Over the next two days Bill guessed they had gone only ten miles, when they should have done fifteen or twenty.

On the third day of snow Bill was standing at Mr.

Simpson's elbow waiting for orders when a mule and rider appeared out of the swirling white. The rider looked like a statue, covered from head to toe in a white frosted glaze. Without waiting to be asked, Bill ran to fetch the man a hot drink and grabbed his own blanket to bring along.

The shivering rider took several minutes wrapped in the blanket and sipping coffee before he could speak.

"Name's Fred Wilson," he said, his voice still a mere gasp. "With John Dawson's outfit."

Bill recognized the wagon master Dawson's name. Lew Simpson's train was only one of forty-one trains that had set out late from Fort Leavenworth heading for Fort Bridger. There were at least seventeen trains ahead of them, one of them Dawson's. They expected most of those had already reached the fort.

"Our train and Bob Barrett's was jumped last night at Simpson's Hollow," Wilson said, still breathing heavily.

"What happened?" Lew Simpson asked sharply.

"It was that Mormon fella, Major Lot Smith they call him, attacked with his militia. They was waiting for us. They outgunned us and ordered us off the wagons. Then they set fire to the lot of 'em."

"They burned both trains?" Mr. Simpson asked, aghast.

"That's right, sir. Fifty wagons gone, burned to

cinders along with everything inside 'em, and the teams caught or driven off. This mule wandered back, and the wagon master ordered me to come lookin' for you, give you the heads up."

"What of the teamsters?" Mr. Simpson asked.

"Smith set 'em afoot, headed toward Camp Winfield. Colonel Alexander's advance guard out of Fort Leavenworth is camped there. There'll be food there, and some kind of shelter. At least half the trains are still out, and I'm instructed to tell you to hold up at Big Sandy Creek and wait for an armed escort. I need to be getting back to Dawson, unless you got a message for him."

Mr. Simpson turned to Bill, his eyes blazing.

"Did you get all that?" he asked. Bill nodded, eyes wide.

"Ride down the line, son, fast as you can. Spread the word. We gonna ride like hell for Big Sandy Creek. Rifles at the ready—we got to be prepared to get the drop on these scoundrels if they jump."

"Yes sir," Bill said, whirling Mike around and taking off toward the closest wagon. If he was scared, he was too cold to feel it.

CHAPTER TEN
BIG SANDY CREEK

★   ★   ★

It was a long way, and the teams were weak. But somehow they reached Big Sandy Creek that same day. They circled the wagons, releasing the exhausted teams into the protected central area. Bill wished they had not left all the beef cattle at Fort Kearny, as ordered. What a difference some fresh steak might make to the men! But he wouldn't let himself think about beef.

Bill set out to gather as many buffalo chips as he could find in the snow for fuel. As he picked through the snow with frozen fingers, he ruefully remembered teasing his sister Julia about buffalo chips. She had stoutly refused to believe that anything that came out of a buffalo's backside and dried up on the grass could be used to make a fire. Even after Pa had assured her it was true, she had looked scandalized. Bill cut the memory short as soon as Pa entered it, and made himself focus completely on the task at hand. The sooner he had a bucketful of chips, the sooner his mess could have their cook fire and some hot grub.

As he did from time to time, Wild Bill Hickok joined their mess that evening. Bill was pleased to see him. He felt tense and helpless, waiting for their army escort to arrive and all the while knowing that their fellow teamsters might still be struggling on foot through the deepening snow toward shelter. Bill scuttled around doing his supper chores, and when he was finished and ready to eat his own supper, there was a place for him next to Wild Bill. Bill no longer felt strange about settling down next to the marksman. The seat was intended for him. He knew that now.

"You expect they'll find us, James?" Bill asked, his mouth mostly full of hot stew.

"I expect somebody will," Wild Bill replied airily. "Army, Indians, or them Danites," which was what some called the Mormons. "We won't be alone for too long. I reckon we're mightly popular about now."

"You don't like the Mormons, do you?" Bill asked.

"Ain't got no quarrel with them," Wild Bill responded. "They been harassed and shooed off on account of their queer ways, and I got a certain measure of sympathy for that. Not everyone wants to live like regular folks, after all. They were in Illinois, you know, in a place called Nauvoo not too long back. Thousands of 'em. But other folks got plenty riled and eventually drove 'em off. That's why they all crossed the plains out to Salt Lake. They figured they could live in peace there, outside of the territories. But since the war with Mexico that land is Utah Territory. Government ain't gonna stand for a settlement that don't follow their laws. That's why they're sending in the army."

Wild Bill rarely spoke so long without stopping. Bill made sure his friend was finished before he spoke.

"What would you do if the Mormons came after us?"

"I wouldn't do nothing but what Lew would have me do. It's his outfit, and he's the boss."

Bill paused.

"But . . ." he began, then he faltered.

"Spit it out, son," said Wild Bill, looking amused.

"I just . . . I mean I sort of figured if it came to it, you'd kind of take over in a fight," Bill said.

"And why would I do that? Like I said, I ain't head of this outfit. I weren't head of Jim Lane's Free Stater army either. He joined me up on account of my being a dead shot, but that didn't make me the big toad in the puddle. I don't reckon Jim Lane woulda taken kindly to my takin' over, as you put it, in a skirmish, and Lew Simpson wouldn't neither. You got to respect the man in charge, Bill, no matter what. Let him lead."

Bill sat thoughtfully, trying to vanquish the thoughts he'd had of Wild Bill Hickok leaping into the fray, firing from both hips and laying waste to whatever enemy dared attack them.

"Simpson's got our backs," Wild Bill continued. "If the army don't find us, he'll get us out somehow. He ain't never lost a man, 'cept for what he killed himself."

Bill wondered, Is that supposed to be comforting?

Ferd was approaching their mess.

"Bill Cody?" he called. "We got to drive these oxen to some water before they sleep. Simpson says he's spotted a stream that ain't too iced over. He wants you to help us herd the teams to drink."

"Yes sir," Bill said, jumping up.

Bill tried not to think how unpleasant it was to walk away from the fire and into the bitter evening. He was no better or worse off than any other man, with his thin coat and worn hat, and just his work gloves to keep his hands covered. Nobody had figured on being caught in the snow. He joined Ferd where he was starting to move the oxen out of the corral, and occasionally rubbed his hands on one of the animals' backs. Covered with snow as they were, the fur didn't give much warmth.

"Ain't no call for you to bother yourself with this," Ferd was saying to Mr. Simpson.

"Aw heck, Ferd, it's easier for me to show you the way than explain so you'll find it in all this snow. Besides, you know how I hate sitting around doing nothing," came Mr. Simpson's voice. It was halfway to dark now, and everything had taken on a strange, bluish light. Bill brought up the rear, slapping the occasional straying ox on the shoulder as he trudged along.

The stream was not far. Bill helped the two men bust holes in the ice, then stepped aside so the oxen could step up and drink their fill. All was quiet except for the sounds of the animals lapping up the water and shifting from hoof to hoof in the snow. Still, something prickled at the back of Bill's neck. He felt . . . watched.

"Mr. Simpson?" Bill asked.

"What is it, son?"

"I . . ." Bill hesitated a moment. But this was no time to worry about the embarrassment of being wrong. If he thought someone was out there, he had to say so.

"It's just a feeling, sir. But I think maybe someone's

on our tail, out here," Bill whispered.

Mr. Simpson's hand went to his six-shooter, and he stood very still.

"I don't hear—" Ferd began, but the wagon master shushed him.

"Who's out there? Show yourself!" Mr. Simpson called. The stream was lined with trees on both sides. In the dimming light any one of them could be hiding a man, or more.

When a figure stepped forward, Bill almost jumped out of his skin.

"Hold up!" Simpson yelled, but the man continued forward. Simpson raised his pistol, but as the man continued to approach, Bill suddenly recognized him as Fred Wilson, the bullwhacker from Dawson's outfit who'd come back to warn them. Bill gave a soft sigh of relief and almost laughed. What had he thought he was going to see?

"Wilson," Mr. Simpson said, lowering his pistol. "Why in land's sake didn't ya just say so? We're kind of jumpy around here, you know."

"Sorry," said Wilson, looking around. "Watering your team, eh?"

"What in tarnation are you doing back here this time o' night?" Mr. Simpson demanded.

"Well . . . I was told to let you know your escort was delayed."

"Delayed? Who told you?"

"My boss," Wilson said, glancing over his shoulder.

"I thought you said your outfit was marching for Camp Winfield."

"Uh-huh," Wilson replied.

"So how'd you have time . . ."

Bill whirled around, suddenly. Something was moving the herd.

Then everyone was shouting at once. Bill and Ferd were both shouting that the oxen were moving off. Simpson was shouting at Wilson, and Wilson was shouting at someone else. And there were other voices, many other voices, none of which Bill recognized. Simpson and Wilson were struggling over the pistol, while six or seven men Bill had never seen before appeared out of nowhere, cracking whips and moving the herd off. Two more men stood at Wilson's back, holding guns. Mr. Simpson, having been made to surrender his pistol, put his hands in the air and stared angrily.

Bill heard a sound like ripping cloth, and the sky glowed pink, then orange. Then he smelled smoke.

"Goddammit, Wilson, what in the hell is happening here?" shouted Mr. Simpson, violating the Majors and Russell profanity rule for the first time in Bill's experience.

"It's Smith, to be honest," the man replied. "Major Lot Smith. My militia will be taking your teams, if you please. And as you can see," he continued, nodding toward the orange glow, "we'll be disposing of that freight. I don't mean to hurt none of you, Simpson, but I can't let those supplies through. You let me do what I must, and I'll leave you and your men be."

They began to move as a group back toward the camp.

"So you jumped them other two trains yourself," Mr. Simpson said, and Major Smith nodded.

"And you burned 'em and set those men off afoot, as you said, toward Camp Winfield?"

"That's right," Major Smith said. He held the gun at his side as he walked, watching Simpson's every move. He did not seem particularly threatened by Bill or Ferd, walking behind him between two other men.

"Well then, it don't sound to me like you 'don't mean to hurt no one,'" Mr. Simpson said angrily. "Those men may be as good as dead. They ain't outfitted to walk through no snowstorm."

"I didn't harm a single man," Major Smith said.

"Well, I'm here to tell you that you did," Mr. Simpson insisted. "And if you mean to do the same to us, you may as well shoot the whole outfit now, get it over with quick."

Bill felt weak in the legs. What was Mr. Simpson doing? Was he actually asking this Mormon to kill them all?

"What would you have me do?" Major Smith said. "I've said I'll do no violence against your people. But I must protect my own, and I can't allow those supplies to reach the army."

"Leave us with one wagon, and one team, to get us to Camp Winfield once you've gone."

Major Smith thought for a moment.

"I might could be persuaded to do that," he said.

"And some provisions, and several weapons. This here is hostile country," Mr. Simpson added quickly.

Major Smith stopped, causing everyone else to stop with him. Bill thought the Mormon might be about to laugh.

"Let me see if I got this straight," Major Smith said. "I just captured you, your outfit, and your oxen. And all I gotta do to keep what I got anyway is give you back a wagon, a team, and some provisions."

"And weapons," Mr. Simpson insisted.

"And weapons," Major Smith repeated.

"This here is hostile country," Mr. Simpson said.

The snow had stopped, and the moon peeked out from a cloud. The two men stood there staring at each other in the bluish light.

"You actually expect me to agree to this?" Major Smith asked.

Mr. Simpson shrugged. "Either you're dealing me straight or you're dealing me dirty. If it's true that you don't mean to harm us, you'll do as I ask and give us a fighting chance. If it ain't true, then shoot us all quick, like I said. I don't care to freeze to death, and I don't reckon my men do neither."

"And in exchange for this, what do I get that I don't already have?" Major Smith asked.

"You get my promise that my men will let you go about your business peaceably. And you convince me that a Mormon is as good as his word," Mr. Simpson replied.

Major Smith gave a look of both amusement and admiration.

"I like you, Simpson," he said. "You're looking out for your own just as I am. I tell you what. You got a deal."

"Thank you," said Mr. Simpson.

Bill almost shouted a hooray, but he followed Ferd's lead and walked quietly into the camp, where five or six of the wagons were already fully ablaze. Smith's milita men, maybe twenty of them, had rounded up the outfit by the lead wagon.

"Now listen up!" Mr. Simpson called. "We been jumped and we're beat. In exchange for a wagon and team, and provisions enough to get us to Camp Winfield, we're gonna stand aside and let these fellas dispose of this freight. I don't want none of you trying anything funny, understand?"

There were nods and calls of understanding. Major Smith gave Mr. Simpson a nod, then began giving orders to his men. Bringing one man with him,

Major Smith walked over to a wagon that was not yet burning, to look inside. Bill recognized it as Clayton Ewell's wagon.

There was so much movement, so much smoke mixed with blowing snow, Bill wasn't sure how he saw it. But his eye fell upon Clayton Ewell, who had drawn a pistol, raised his arm, and was aiming cleanly at the back of Major Smith's head.

Bill yelled, but the air wasn't even halfway out of his lungs when a shot rang out.

"*No!*" Bill cried. But Major Smith was still standing where he'd been, looking back toward Ewell with a look of confusion. Ewell was bent halfway over, clasping his left hand around his right. His pistol lay on the ground ten feet away.

Bill turned around and looked behind him. Wild Bill Hickok was calmly returning his six-shooter to his holster just as Simpson and Major Smith had gotten their pistols out of their holsters. Though he'd heard the stories, Bill couldn't imagine how Wild Bill could move so fast. Major Smith was staring at Hickok.

"Who's your marksman?" Smith asked Simpson.

"They call him Wild Bill Hickok," Simpson replied. And Bill knew that Wild Bill's fame would now reach Utah Territory.

It was about the worst thing that could happen to a bull outfit, short of dying. They had lost all their freight, and they would arrive at Camp Winfield with little but the clothes on their backs, if they even survived. The odds were still against them, in spite of the wagon and team Smith was letting them keep. They could all freeze to death this very night.

But Bill had just seen Wild Bill Hickok shoot the pistol out of another man's hand at forty paces through moonlit smoke and snow.

He had to believe that anything was possible.

CHAPTER ELEVEN

CAMP WINFIELD

★   ★   ★

They rode most of the way in silence, cramped in the back of the wagon. Only about half of them could fit comfortably, so those who felt up to it took turns walking for a spell to make more room, and Mr. Simpson himself drove the team, walking alongside it with his blacksnake. The wagon master and Wild Bill had been allowed to keep their pistols. All of the other rifles had been taken. Lot Smith had said with a laugh that he guessed nothing was gonna get by Hickok's six-shooter, and one pistol on top of that one oughtta be enough. Mr. Simpson had no choice but to agree.

It would be at least a two-day trip to the army's encampment. Bill chose to walk for the time being. The morning was bright, and the sun warmed his face. The team and wagon squashed a flat path through the snow. As he walked over it, thoughts of his pa kept flitting through his mind. Pa pointing out the site of their new claim in Salt Creek Valley. Pa clearing their new fields. Pa riding alongside Bill to Fort Leavenworth the day he got stabbed. Pa leaving for Grasshopper Falls when the border ruffians threatened to finish him off. He tried to get mad by thinking of Major Lot Smith jumping them. But it wasn't working.

The more Bill tried to swat the thoughts away, the more insistently they came to him. What was the matter with him? Was he going crazy? He tried to focus on his footsteps, on the height of the snow drifts, on anything but his pa. But nothing worked. When he heard footsteps behind him, he glanced back and actually *saw* Pa walking behind him. Bill let out a little shout.

Of course it wasn't Pa at all. It was only Hiram Cummings.

"You all right, son?" Hiram asked.

Bill nodded, then quickened his pace to avoid any

more questions. He must be going crazy. He was growing more sure of it by the minute. His heart was hammering, and in spite of the cold his hands felt hot and sweaty. Bill was suddenly gripped with the fear that he was going to die. What else could be rattling him so?

The more he thought about it, the crazier he felt. Everyone just kept walking along like nothing was wrong, but surely they knew Bill was acting odd. They must. Bill looked behind him. There were ten or so men walking, spread out in a column behind the wagon. Bill knew that Hickok was one of them; the marksman never rode when he could walk. And yes, there he was, about six men back and walking by himself. For a moment Bill wanted to run to him, to get his help. But this would not be the manly thing to do. Bill did not want to scamper like a child to Wild Bill Hickok when things were amiss.

No, he could not talk to Wild Bill. But maybe there was no harm in *imagining* he was talking to him. Heck, if he was going crazy anyway, why not have a conversation in his head with someone who wasn't actually talking to him?

He tried to picture Wild Bill's face. He tried to imagine himself talking to him, and Wild Bill talking back. But it was no use. He might be crazy, but he wasn't crazy enough to get an imaginary person to talk back to him. All right, then. Instead of trying to talk to Wild Bill, Bill would try to imagine what Wild Bill might *do* if he were in the same situation. How would he handle himself?

Again, Bill seemed to come up with nothing. Except that one word kept coming to his mind, and that word was *story*. Wild Bill had talked about everyone having his own story. It was the stories that made up all the people, helped them understand each other. I got my own story, Bill thought ruefully. I just never told it.

Bill stopped suddenly. He had never told his story. He wouldn't even let it into his own head. If what Wild Bill said was right, maybe Bill wasn't ever going to feel like himself until he gave that story a voice. Bill started walking again. It didn't take long for thoughts of Pa to come knocking again. This time Bill tried letting them in.

After they'd finished eating their supper, the men in Bill's mess sat close together around the fire. It was just too cold to do anything else. Everyone looked wrung out, particularly Hank. Bill pretended to have a sour stomach and offered Hank his ration of bacon. It took a few minutes to convince Hank he really wasn't able to eat it before Hank finally accepted the extra food.

"What's a young grasshopper like you doing with a bad stomach anyhow?" Hank asked. "Something bothering you?"

It was a funny question. They were out in the snow, tired, freezing, and miles from shelter, and Hank wanted to know if something was bothering Bill. But he answered the question seriously.

"Oh, I don't know. I been thinking about my pa today."

He'd said it. He'd mentioned Pa.

"You must be missing him," Hank said. When Bill opened his mouth to speak, there were so many words suddenly fighting to get out, he expected to be talking gibberish. But instead he spoke clearly.

"I do miss him. I guess I never really expected he was gonna die. After the border ruffians stabbed him, he was never real healthy again. But he'd be sick and then he'd be okay awhile. He had good months and bad months. When he took sick in the winter, I thought he'd get better like he always did. But he kept getting thinner and his cough got worse, and he couldn't get out of bed at all anymore. Then one day he called me in by myself. I guess I must have known then he was fixing to die."

Bill paused. Hank waited, listening. Hiram, Ferd, and several others were also watching Bill now, waiting for him to continue.

"He didn't say much, just asked me to take care of things as best I could. Told me he had faith in me. And then he was too tired to talk anymore. Not too long after, Ma came in and brought my sisters in with her. Read some of his favorite psalms and such like. Pa had looked like he was sleeping, but then all of the sudden he opened his eyes, looking surprised, and he said, 'I see Sammy!' After that he didn't breathe no more."

Bill stopped. He was finished. There was a momentary silence.

"Who did he mean, when he said he saw Sammy?" asked Hiram.

"My brother Sammy died three years ago," Bill explained. "I figured Pa just got confused."

"Some folks say the dead come back to help the dying pass on," Hank said. "Maybe your pa wasn't confused."

Bill didn't say anything else, but Hank's comment stayed with him. The thought of it was like the moon, bright and hopeful, if too distant to grasp.

Midway through the next day, Mr. Simpson called out to the men that Camp Winfield was in sight.

The first thing Bill felt was disappointment. *Camp Winfield* had a cozy sound to it. But there was nothing cozy about this mass of bedraggled men and animals. The group was a mixture of soldiers and freighters, wagons and tents, arranged in several rough circles. All around, in the snow, Bill could see the bodies of dead oxen, some of which were being cut up for meat. The oxen must have starved to death,

Bill thought. There was nowhere left to graze.

For months, Bill had been part of a group of thirty-one men. Now, they were joining the more than two thousand soldiers forming the Army of Utah from Fort Leavenworth and the Majors & Russell bullwhackers from other trains at the camp, none of whom were in very good shape. It was an unpleasant adjustment. Bill felt lost in the huge camp, and he did not understand why they were there. Accustomed as he was to following orders without question, Bill had been several hours helping to set up their own small camp before he had a chance to ask what was going on.

"Hank? How come we didn't go to Fort Bridger? How come we're all staying out here? Why are there soldiers here?" Bill asked. Hank was a great one for ferreting out information, and he always had the latest developments.

"'Cause there ain't no more Fort Bridger," Hank said. He'd collected the teamsters' few remaining supplies, mostly pots and blankets, and had organized them into a kind of makeshift galley for Green.

"What do you mean? What happened to it?" Bill asked. He dumped the buffalo chips he'd collected into a pile, and now he and Hank bent over and carefully got a fire started.

"Mormons burned it," Hank said. "See, Fort Bridger ain't actually an army post. Leastwise it wasn't—reckon maybe they'll put one there now. Jim

Bridger opened it as a trading post in forty-three after he retired from trapping. I suppose you already know that."

Bill nodded. Like any boy with ears on both sides of his head, he'd heard plenty about the legendary Jim Bridger, the West's most famous mountain man, trapper, and scout.

"But that was a coon's age back," said Bill. Fort Bridger had been established four years before he'd even been born. "You don't mean he's still trading there after all these years?"

Hank allowed a small grin.

"Well no, Bill, I do not," he said. "Jim Bridger left these parts some years back. Some say he sold his fort to the Mormons, and others say the Mormons up and drove him off the land. But it's the Mormons been using Fort Bridger ever since. And when they heard the army was heading their way, they burned it to the ground before taking to their heels."

"What is the army supposed to do when it's in Utah Territory?" Bill asked.

"Well, Bill, the colonel don't tell me everything," Hank said with a little wink. "I know there's been trouble between the government and the Mormons for years. There's supposed to be a new governor in Utah Territory, to replace that Mormon fella Brigham Young. Maybe they sent the army to make sure the new governor gets listened to. Mormons like to be governed by their own, and they don't cotton to outsiders. I figure the government expected trouble replacing Brigham Young, and they decided to take the bull by the horns and send the army along. Though the way things look now," Hank added, looking around at the desolate, snowy scene, "it's more like we've got the bull by the tail. We can't stay here for long, no matter how burned the fort the army planned to use is. There's no more grazing here, and these animals are gonna keep dying. I suppose we won't starve as we can eat *them*, but I sure don't fancy spending too many nights in this kind o' weather."

"What do you suppose it is we're waiting *for*?" asked Bill. The fire was burning decently now. Bill held his hands, stinging from the cold, toward the warmth.

"Word is Colonel Johnston ain't arrived yet. He set out from Leavenworth with the rear army later than the dragoons. Don't suppose anybody can do anything until he shows up. We're just gonna have to sit tight. World has come to a sad pass when only a bucketful of buffalo chips is standing atween us and freezing."

Hank must have noticed Bill's frown, for he quickly added, "Not that anybody's gonna seriously take ill with a camp full of dragoons and a prairie full of meat offering itself up to us. I just elect for comfort whenever possible, and I ain't comfortable, Bill Cody. And you ain't either, unless you feel like lying."

Bill smiled. He was glad of Hank's company, but the news that Fort Bridger had burned worried him. For the last two months, Bill's entire life had been about freighting a train full of supplies to Fort Bridger. Now he found that on top of losing the train, they'd lost the fort, too.

Bill felt a flash of anger. Then he almost laughed out loud at his own selfishness. He was angry, he realized, because he'd been looking forward to seeing the famous Fort Bridger. He wanted to return to Salt Creek Valley and say to the others, "Well, when I was up at Fort Bridger . . ." How could anyone have gone and burned such a famous place?

"I reckon maybe it's a good thing Jim Bridger didn't live to see the day when his fort got burned down by the Mormons," Bill said solemnly.

"What nonsense are you talking, Bill?" Hank asked, leaning over to blow a little on the fire.

"Ain't he dead?" Bill asked. Hank looked up and rolled his eyes.

"Pups," he said. "They all think we die soon as we git forty. Not only ain't he dead, Bill, but fact is he just walked past you."

Now it was Bill's turn to roll his eyes. But Hank simply stood up straight and pointed. Bill looked.

An old, weathered-looking man as skinny as a

string bean and as gray as a storm cloud had stopped at the next mess over. Wild Bill Hickok was saying something to him, and the old man listened while looking across the camp. His eyes never seemed to stop moving. Bill supposed there wasn't any reason he *wasn't* Jim Bridger. Except that Bill didn't see why a legend like Jim Bridger would be in this miserable place.

"You're full of gum, Hank," Bill said. Hank shrugged.

"What would Jim Bridger come here for?" Bill pressed.

"Army hired him to scout the way," Hank said. "No man knows the way to Fort Bridger better."

Bill wanted to believe Hank so badly, he could taste it. But Hank loved a good joke, and Bill figured he was being set up for one.

"I don't believe you," Bill said.

"Suit yourself," Hank replied. "Don't make any difference to me what you believe."

Bill picked up his empty bucket, hesitated, then sauntered casually toward the place the old man was standing. When he got within ten feet, Bill suddenly became very interested in something on the ground. He put his bucket down and stared at the snow. He picked his bucket up. He put it down again.

The third time he picked his bucket up, he saw with a start that the old man and Wild Bill had started walking, and they were going to pass right by where Bill was standing and fidgeting. Bill started to put the bucket down again but lost his nerve. He thought the pair was going to walk on by him without even noticing he was standing there. But at the last minute Wild Bill slowed up.

"Oh, here's my friend Bill Cody. Bill, this here is Jim Bridger," Wild Bill said.

The old man paused and looked at Bill with sharp, blue eyes.

"Mr. Bridger," Bill heard himself say politely. His voice seemed to be coming from a great distance away—say, somewhere around Oregon Territory.

"Bill," the old man responded with a nod. Bill saw the flash of teeth as Wild Bill shot him a grin; then the two walked off.

Bill grasped the handle of his bucket with both hands. He would have to keep this bucket now, as a souvenir. This bucket had come within three feet of Jim Bridger! Bill was in utter awe of himself. He hardly knew what to do first.

Seeing Hank still standing by the fire heating up a pot of coffee, Bill rushed over to him.

"Hank, Hank!" Bill cried, almost gasping for breath. "You ain't gonna *believe* who I just met!"

CHAPTER TWELVE

JOURNEY'S END

★   ★   ★

It was three long, uncomfortable weeks before Colonel Johnston arrived at Camp Winfield. The men began to pack up that same day. Word spread quickly, and Bill soon learned that the colonel would be leading an advance party of his soldiers to Fort Bridger. They were to begin rebuilding the fort immediately, this time as a military structure. Jim Bridger had originally chosen the ground for his fort in a most strategic area at Black's Fork on the Green River, where the trail split to

Oregon in one direction and California on the other. The army would need it now in the dispute with the Mormons. The remainder of the men, along with what oxen and wagons had gotten through intact, would follow.

The journey was miserable from the start. So many oxen had died, there were hardly enough to pull the remaining wagons. Seven Majors & Russell trains had reached Camp Winfield intact, and Colonel Johnston had escorted in another ten when he arrived. Most had to make do with only two yokes of oxen to pull, half the usual number. The teams in the rear of the column fared the worst—there was seldom anything left for them to graze on. Oxen could live well on grass and plants, but they needed to be constantly moving to have a fresh supply. What could be eaten through the snow was long since gone. Bill figured that there was never more than an hour in each day before another animal fell to its knees, paused as if to contemplate the struggle, then pitched over dead. Each time this happened, the dead animal had to be unhitched from the yoke and dragged to the side, a task that required fifteen men and a strong stomach. Bill got to thinking about Mike, who had been stampeded off along with the oxen at Big Sandy Creek. He hoped the mule had enough to eat.

By the end of the first week there were no longer enough teams to pull all the wagons at the same time. Mr. Simpson told the men they would be going in two shifts from now on. Half the wagons would move forward a mile. Then the teams would be unhitched, walked back to the remainder of the party, and rehitched. Bill thought he'd never heard a worse plan in his life. It was like moving a haystack one piece of straw at a time! But he had to admit he could think of no better way himself. One way or another they all had to get to what was left of Fort Bridger and help rebuild it. With all they had lost, they could not afford to leave a single wagon behind. Each wagon would be taken apart and its wood used to help erect the new fort.

By midway through the second week Bill had stopped counting the days. When they were on the move, at least, they could get warm by going afoot for a spell. And just the feeling that they were inching closer to their destination was settling. But when they had to stop and wait, it was agony. Word was fights were breaking out right and left, though none took place among Mr. Simpson's men. Worst of all, Hank Bassett had become gravely ill. One day he'd been his usual cheerful though tired self, and the next he'd clutched his chest and fallen in a heap in the snow. The men made him as comfortable as they could in the wagon.

Bill rode in the wagon from then on, sitting by Hank's head. He gave him water and bits of food when the man would allow it. But mostly Hank seemed too weak to do anything but lie there. He began to get a distant look in his eyes that Bill found uncomfortably familiar from Pa's last weeks. Bill would not give up on Hank, though. When he wasn't tending to him, he talked, telling bright stories of his boyhood days in Iowa. He didn't know if it was helping, but he didn't know what else to do, and none of the other teamsters told him to stop.

In the end there was no triumphant arrival. Being in the second detail, the one the teams went back for once they'd pulled the first ahead, Bill knew for a full day and a half that they were closing in on Fort Bridger. When they finally approached its stone wall, Bill barely gave the fort a glance. Though he had imagined this moment many times over the last several months, he felt no happiness. They had nothing, and they were coming to nothing, for every wooden structure within the walls had been destroyed. The rebuilding had already begun, but it was too late for many, including Hank Bassett, who'd died quietly the night before.

Bill would never have believed the first thing he'd do at Fort Bridger was make a man's grave. But that is exactly what he found himself doing. Hank would not be able to have a proper burial until spring, because the ground was frozen solid and would have broken a shovel right in half.

Instead, Bill collected as many big rocks as he

could find. Ferd, Hiram, and Wild Bill hauled in rocks too, all three of them grim and quiet in the bitter wind. Bill placed Hank's hat carefully on the dead man's head and then began placing the rocks on top of the body, as gently as though he were covering a child with a blanket.

He wouldn't rest until the pile of rocks was almost three feet high. You had to be careful, Bill knew, to make the grave fortified. He'd passed too many shallow graves on the trail that had been raided by wolves or coyotes, the remains drawn out and left on the ground. He would never let that happen to Hank.

The outfit's carpenter made a grave marker out of two halves of a broken wagon wheel. Bill himself carved the words in:

Hank Bassett 1814–1857
M & R bull outfit wagon 27
A fine bullwhacker and a good friend

Every man in the outfit, even Clayton Ewell, stood around the gravesite while Mr. Simpson read a Bible passage and offered a remembrance of Hank. Then, one by one, the men walked off, until only Bill was left behind.

He stayed alone by the grave for the better part of an hour. He was running every joke and tall tale of Hank's he could remember through his head. It was important that he remember everything he could.

That way, Hank would live on as part of Bill's story.

Then Bill put his hat on and got back to work.

Bill did not think about much, other than Hank, those first two or three days. He hauled timber to the building sites. He tended fire at mealtimes and slept when he wasn't doing anything else. There were quarters for the men now, framed with wood and covered with canvas from the wagons, so everyone slept with a roof over his head. By the fourth day Bill's senses began to reawaken. A hunting detail returned with two elk, which were soon cooking over a fire. Given the worsening weather, the elk were probably the last fresh meat the men would have that winter. The portions were small, but Bill savored every bite.

After supper that night, Mr. Simpson sought Bill out. Bill was seeing to his bedding, which was really just a blanket and a half and a bit of old sacking stretched out on the dirt floor of the halfway-finished quarters. The wagon trains were continuing to roll in daily, and most were taken apart for their wood, but timber was still in short supply. It would be some time before anyone could look forward to real bunks in these quarters, which would become part of the permanent fort.

"Evening, Bill," said Mr. Simpson. He looked tired and drawn.

"Evening, Mr. Simpson," Bill replied. "Is there

something needs doing?"

"Not at all, Bill," Mr. Simpson said. "You done quite enough for one day. That's one of the reasons I'm here—ain't had a minute before now. But I wanted to tell you, son, I been a wagon master now for almost ten years, and you're the best extra hand I ever hired on."

Bill glowed with the compliment. Mr. Simpson did not praise lightly or without good reason; everybody knew that.

"I don't know how many wagons will be left to take back east in the spring. But somehow or other we'll get home to Leavenworth, and I need to start thinking about next season. I'm one bullwhacker short now, and I'd like you to be that man," he said. "With all according raises in pay."

Bill swallowed. Bullwhackers made fifty dollars a month—twice what he was making now. But it wasn't the prospect of the additional money that made his ears burn red. Mr. Simpson thought he was ready to be a bullwhacker, and that meant something. It meant everything. Of course, the added pleasure of imagining Ma's face when Bill told her his wages would be doubled didn't hurt.

"Thank you, Mr. Simpson," he said. "I . . ."

"Go on, son," the wagon master prompted.

"I . . . being in the outfit . . . I'm just glad to be on the job," Bill stammered. Mr. Simpson nodded.

"Glad to hear it," he said.

Bill remembered how in awe he'd been of the wagon master the first day he'd seen him back at Fort Leavenworth. Bill had been such a tenderfoot then. He hadn't known how to do a single thing, practically. Now he was an old hand, and soon he'd be a real bullwhacker, too. Fifty dollars a month was a fair living. Ma would not be able to argue against him taking it.

"One other thing, Bill," said Mr. Simpson. He reached around his back and pulled out a blacksnake he'd fastened to his belt.

"This was Hank Bassett's," he said. "It really belongs to Majors and Russell, but I'm taking it on myself to give it to you, Bill. I want you to have it, and Hank would too. Besides, when you start driving your own team, you'll need a blacksnake."

Bill stood ramrod straight with pride as he took the whip from Mr. Simpson.

"Thank you," he said.

"All right then," said Mr. Simpson. He got up and left without another word. It was probably the longest conversation he'd had with Bill since the day they'd met.

Bill sat on his blanket and ran his hands over the whip's worn leather handle. It was shiny and soft where Hank's hand had gripped it every day. Bill fitted his hand around the soft place. Maybe Hank had small hands, or maybe Bill's hands were getting bigger. Either way, the handle fit in his hand like it had been made for him.

He looked around. A few men had filtered into the quarters, and more would soon be coming. Bill coiled the blacksnake, put on his hat, and went quickly outside. Near the cluster of buildings was a half-built enclosure that would eventually be used for the surviving livestock. Colonel Johnston had now moved all but two companies of soldiers up to Willow Creek, several miles away, where they were establishing a second fort. Left with only a few hundred soldiers and bullwhackers, Fort Bridger, now partly rebuilt, seemed larger and more substantial. It also seemed quiet and peaceful.

The temperature was numbingly cold, but there was very little breeze, and the moon shone so brightly, Bill could see his own shadow. He walked to the very edge of the enclosure, by the seven-foot-high stone wall the Mormons had built around the fort after they took it over from Jim Bridger. At least they couldn't burn that down, Bill thought. It was a good, sturdy wall, and Bill was glad someone else had built it.

Bill looked around to make sure he was alone. Sentries were posted, of course, but they were watching for trouble outside the walls, not within. He took the whip from his belt and held it in his hand. Of course, like anyone who'd spent more than five minutes among the bullwhackers, Bill had heard his share of stories of first-time blacksnake crackers. Hank Bassett himself had delighted in telling the tale of one young tenderfoot who had raised his new whip in the air and snapped it forward, only to pluck the hat from the head of a passing lady. Or the greenhorn who'd wrapped his whip around his own neck and almost throttled himself. Bill could almost hear Hank's bellowing laughter filling the night around Fort Bridger.

He raised his arm, still smiling at the thought of watched far too many bullwhackers crack their blacksnakes to make such a blunder of his first try. However, before he could prove himself, a hand closed around his wrist from behind.

"Don't do it," came Wild Bill Hickok's smooth voice. Bill lowered his arm and turned around.

"You ought to know better than to make a sound like a gunshot when you got a load of jumpy dragoons on watch with their guns loaded," Wild Bill said.

Bill suddenly felt more foolish than any greenhorn who'd almost strangled himself with his own blacksnake. Of course, Wild Bill was right. Where was his common sense?

"Sorry," Bill said. "I wasn't thinking."

"Thinking is a highly overrated act," replied Wild Bill. "But I do find, on occasion, that it is a necessary one."

"I never actually cracked a blacksnake before," Bill explained. "Mr. Simpson gave me Hank's."

Wild Bill nodded. He didn't seem surprised.

"I sure didn't figure things would be like this," Bill said.

"Like what?" asked Wild Bill. His face looked oddly angled and shadowed in the moonlight.

"Getting here with almost nothing, the fort gone. Hank dead," Bill said. "I knew it would be hard work crossing the plains. But I never thought we'd end up failing."

"How do you figure we failed, Bill?" asked Wild Bill. "I don't know about you, but I didn't fail at nothing."

"Well . . ." Bill began.

"What were you aiming to do when you set out from Fort Leavenworth?" asked Wild Bill.

"I was aiming to go with the outfit to Fort Bridger. And to be the best extra hand the outfit ever had," Bill replied.

"Well then, it seems to me you ought to be right pleased with yourself," Wild Bill said.

It was true. Put that way, Bill had to agree. He had done what he set out to do.

"Are you going to join up again next season?" asked Bill.

Wild Bill looked thoughtfully into the darkness.

"I couldn't say," he said after a while. "I never make plans that far ahead."

"But you'll stay at Fort Bridger until spring, won't you?" Bill asked, feeling suddenly anxious. He wasn't ready to see Wild Bill go.

"Never make plans that far ahead," Wild Bill repeated. It sounded more like a suggestion than an answer the second time around. The answer frustrated Bill. What was wrong with making plans? He wanted to know Wild Bill was going to be around. Wild Bill's friendship made life more exciting, and now that Bill was comfortable with it, he didn't want to think about letting it go.

"Nothing ever stays the same long enough for me to get used to it," Bill said. He knew it sounded like a complaint, but he couldn't help it. He didn't want Wild Bill Hickok to be another Horace Billings. Horace had twice ridden into Bill's life and made everything interesting and simple. But when Horace had decided to go, he was gone. Was Wild Bill going to be the same way?

"If things always stayed the same, I reckon none of us would ever go out looking for something different," Wild Bill said. "Sometimes you gotta go find life, if it won't come find you."

"Well, how's a person supposed to know where to look?" Bill asked, annoyed. Wild Bill had an answer for everything, and so what if he was just about always right? It was still vexing. "Wouldn't it be my luck to be looking in Nebraska when my life's waiting around for me in Oregon Territory."

Wild Bill just laughed.

"I guess you better make sure and keep moving, then," he said, as he began to head back to the quarters. "That's what I do."

And Bill realized that, of course, he could never hope to keep Wild Bill in his life. He would go, and perhaps their paths would cross over each other. Maybe their paths would cross time and again, so often that they became part and parcel of each other's stories. In the meantime, maybe he should make sure and keep moving. He'd not had any better advice.

Bill smiled as he rubbed his hands over his arms. The cold numbed his limbs and stung his face. He could hardly wait to get inside and under his blanket. And something was poking uncomfortably into his leg. He reached into his pocket and pulled out Julia's letter. If he got a spot close enough to the fireplace in the quarters, there would be enough light to read it tonight.

But he stayed outside just a few moments longer, listening to Wild Bill's footsteps fade. Bill looked around at the moonlit scene. The fort was being rebuilt from the ground up. All it took was some wood and nails and plenty of manpower. It would not be the same as it had been before. Nothing ever was.

But with any luck, it would be better.

AFTERWORD

Bill's adventures in this book, and in the first three books in the Buffalo Bill series, are all soundly based in fact. But as Bill reached his twelfth year, events and dates in his life become confused.

According to Bill's own autobiography, he joined Majors & Russell in 1857 as an extra hand in time to participate in the ill-fated freighting trip to Fort Bridger, when wagon master Lew Simpson's train was attacked and burned by the Mormons. In fact, Bill gives a highly detailed account of that trip, including his first meeting with Wild Bill Hickok, who saved him from being bullied by another teamster. The expedition itself, including the capture and destruction of the wagon train, is all historical fact. However, not everyone agrees that Bill Cody and Wild Bill Hickok were actually there.

It is certain that Bill worked as an extra hand on a freighting trip at some point after his pa died, and Bill recounts several different cross-plains journeys in his autobiography. Scholars guess those journeys took place sometime between 1857 and 1859. I have chosen certain elements from those stories and combined them to form one journey for the purposes of this book. Alexander Majors and Lew Simpson are both real men, as is Jim Bridger, but Bill's bullwhacker companions, such as Hank Bassett, Hiram Cummings, and Clayton Ewell, are fictional characters.

Whether it was in 1857 or one or two years later, Bill did meet Wild Bill Hickok on one of his trips over the plains, and the two men became lifelong friends. Of everyone Bill had encountered in his life, only Wild Bill Hickok would achieve the kind of legendary status and fame that Bill himself would come to know as Buffalo Bill Cody. But unlike Buffalo Bill, Wild Bill Hickok's life was cut short. Only thirty-nine years old, he was shot and killed while playing poker in Deadwood, Dakota Territory. In death he became even more famous than he had been in life.

Bill would continue to do a man's work to help support his ma and five siblings (Martha having married John Crane and moved away). Though he would return to his home often, he was constantly on the move. Through his autobiography we follow him through Majors & Russell's Pony Express, to work as a scout in the Civil War, to buffalo hunter, and beyond. As the Wild West of Bill's youth grew tamer with the advent of civilization and the coming of the railroad, Bill turned his talents to his Wild West Show, where he re-created the stories of the old West that had captured the world's imagination.

Like all stories, they got better with every telling.